"I take it you're still . . . upset?"

"In what capacity are you asking? As wagon master, official mediator, curious bystander, or—"

"As a friend, Johanna," Freddy replied. "And as of this moment, you won't have to do all of these chores alone. I'm going to be your new roommate."

"What?" She gave him an incredulous stare.

"No one—man or woman—travels alone in my wagon train. It's the rule. I know you have a dependable driver to handle your team during the day, but you need someone here in the evenings . . . and through the night." Freddy folded his arms across his chest. "I'll be that someone. You can trust me, Johanna."

"Oh, my God," she whispered beneath her breath. Last night she had vowed to test her own strength and independence no matter what the consequences. Freddy's constant presence was certainly going to put a kink in her plans. Johanna felt the heat rush to her face as she raised her eyes to meet the dark intensity of his gaze. "I think I'd rather chance the wild animals, Mr. Rotini."

Jamisan Whitney

Jamisan Whitney grew up in a large family on the Oregon coast and began writing illustrated stories for classmates in the first grade. She won a national poetry contest at the age of nine and went on to publish nonfiction, short stories, and poetry while earning degrees in journalism and communications.

After more than a decade of juggling concurrent careers as a free-lance photographer and a television writer/producer, Jamisan began writing romantic fiction full time. A five-week journey through the American Southwest resulted in Driven to Distraction, *her first sale to Second Chance at Love. When a sequel was suggested, she chose the heroine's brother, Freddy Rotini, for* Desire's Destiny, *because he shared Jamisan's gypsy soul and love of philosophy.*

Despite her *gypsy soul, Jamisan is currently settled in Seattle, where she enjoys watching sunsets with her husband, Jerry "J.C." Chan, who works in broadcasting and critiques all of her writing.*

Romantic Times *magazine made Jamisan the first recipient of their WISH Award in 1987. The award is presented to contemporary authors for the portrayal of a memorable hero.*

Other Second Chance at Love books by
Jamisan Whitney

DRIVEN TO DISTRACTION #315
HEAVEN SENT #423

Dear Reader:

We're pleased to announce that the winner of our "*Gamble* sweepstakes," which we told you about in our August 1987 letter, is Mrs. Mary Koenig of Phoenix, Arizona. Mrs. Koenig tells us she's been reading Second Chance at Love romances since we began publishing the series in 1981, and her favorite authors include Carole Buck, Jackie Leigh, Cait Logan, and Courtney Ryan. We're sending a personally inscribed, autographed copy of the bestselling historical romance *The Gamble* by LaVyrle Spencer to Mrs. Koenig, and also to her romance bookseller, Mr. Joe Canas, assistant manager of the Waldenbooks store at the Thomas Mall in Phoenix. Congratulations, Mrs. Koenig and Mr. Canas!

Sherryl Woods and Jamisan Whitney, the authors of our January releases, will keep you in stitches with their own distinctive brands of humor. The winner of the 1986 *Romantic Times* Reviewer's Choice "Pink Fuzzy" award, for the author most likely to cheer readers on a rainy day, Sherryl's created a rollicking comedy about a heroine whose search for Mr. Right produces delightfully surprising results. And Jamisan, the first winner of *Romantic Times*'s WISH (Women in Search of a Hero) award, wonderfully satisfies your requests for a spin-off from her first, critically acclaimed romance, *Driven to Distraction* (#315).

If you've ever placed or answered a Personals ad—or wanted to—you'll especially enjoy *Prince Charming Replies* (#430) by Sherryl Woods. Single parent Katie Stewart advertises for Prince Charming and arranges to meet the most promising respondents—and then her gorgeous boss, Ross Chandler, unexpectedly begins to court her! The other men in her life pique Ross's jealousy, and yet another suitor appears—a secret admirer who writes Katie ever-so-romantic letters. Suddenly, she's so besieged by men, her head's awhirl ... but her heart recognizes her true Prince Charming. *Prince Charming Replies,* Sherryl's sixth Second Chance at Love novel, offers romantic entertainment at its finest—full of warmth, humor, and as much sparkle as the Hope diamond!

Desire's Destiny (#431), Jamisan Whitney's third Second Chance at Love romance, balances laugh-out-loud comedy and emotional depth as philosopher/truck driver Freddy Rotini loses his heart to historian Johanna Remington on the Oregon Trail. Jamisan's created some hilariously memorable secondary characters, like eccentric Charlie Vishtek, who lost his wagon train to Freddy in a poker game, and Charlie's pretentious son, James. Thor and Andee Engborg, the hero and heroine of Jamisan's first romance, appear here, too. Indeed, Andee gives birth during a dramatic scene in which Johanna confronts and conquers her past, freeing herself from the last obstacle to her love for Freddy.

This month we're offering a particularly outstanding selection of longer fiction for you to read on those snowy and sub-freezing days when a good book seems a godsend. For you Judith Michaels fans, we highly recommend first novel *Mirror, Mirror* by Betsy von Furstenberg, an enthralling story about two half-sisters who experience passion and scandal, jealousy and betrayal, amid the glamor of Venice, Paris, and the Bahamas. Bestselling author Barbara Michaels delivers a tour de force of romantic suspense in *Shattered Silk,* and another of our bestselling authors, Shannon Drake—aka Heather Graham Pozzessere—weaves a fascinating web of desire and danger in 17th-century England in *Ondine.* We're also publishing a new Barbara Cartland novel, *Sapphires in Siam,* and a new giant-size Regency by Elizabeth Mansfield, *A Grand Deception.* We're reissuing Georgette Heyer's Regency *Sprig Muslin,* and Mary Westmacott's novel of romantic intrigue *The Rose and the Yew Tree.* You're probably more familiar with Mary Westmacott's other pen name, Agatha Christie, whose mystery *The Murder at Hazelmoor* we're also reissuing in January. Our other mysteries by women writers include *The Doom Campaign* by award-winning author Mary McMullen, *Enter a Murderer* by the renowned Ngaio Marsh; and Heron Carvic's *Witch Miss Seeton,* the launch book of a delightful series that we're publishing in paperback for the first time—we'll be publishing a new Miss Seeton mystery every three months, and they're sure to appeal to all you devotees of Miss Marple and Miss Silver.

As always, we wish you happy reading!

Sincerely,

Joan Marlow

Joan Marlow, Editor
SECOND CHANCE AT LOVE
The Berkley Publishing Group
200 Madison Avenue
New York, NY 10016

SECOND CHANCE AT LOVE™

JAMISAN WHITNEY

DESIRE'S DESTINY

For Jill —
Good luck on your
writing career —
persevere & believe in
yourself —
All my best
Norma Brownlie
aka
Jamisan Whitney

BERKLEY BOOKS, NEW YORK

First edition published January 1988

ISBN: 0-425-10605-5

Second Chance at Love books are published by
The Berkley Publishing Group
200 Madison Avenue, New York, NY 10016

Printed in the United States of America

10 9 8 7 6 5 4 3 2 1

Dedicated to my father and mother,
R. V. and Lenora Brownlie,
(it's time to admit I was always your favorite)

and my sisters and brother,
Beth, Margaret, Michael, LaVonne,
Mary Kaye, and Teresa,
who share a treasured legacy of love
and laughter.

PROLOGUE

TEN ACTION-PACKED days of adventure on the Oregon Trail. Follow the path of pioneers in a covered wagon! Enjoy cookouts, square dancing, horseback riding, hiking, and fishing. Sing songs and share folklore around a real campfire. Experienced crew. Balanced diet. Gentle horses. Philosophy majors most welcome. For more information and applications, contact wagon master Freddy Rotini, RIDE THE OREGON TRAIL WAGON TREK, in care of Andee Rotini-Engborg, Taos, New Mexico.

Freddy sat forward, rested his chin in the palm of one hand, and studied his ad in the *Getaway Guide* for the third time. "You've really done it this time, Rotini," he berated himself aloud. Standing up, he paced his sister's spacious living room as he continued to mutter, "For a man who doesn't know diddly-squat about the Oregon Trail, you're in deep. *Too* deep!"

He paced back to the sofa and landed on the cushions with a loud groan. There was no way he could back out now. The ads had been published, interested parties had returned their applications, and it was early April. The first of several ten-day treks would start in mid-May, and it was time to decide which applicants would be aboard.

Freddy looked over the five piles of correspondence on the coffee table. He had categorized them carefully in an effort to select a harmonious mixture of people for what could be a long ten days. He was drawn to a letter from the last pile. There were several envelopes in the group he had mentally labeled "intellectuals/snobs."

> Dear Mr. Rotini,
>
> I saw your ad in *Western History Digest* and my interest was piqued. I sent for your application, which I've filled out and enclosed. Let me introduce myself. My name is Johanna Remington. I've taught history of the Western United States at the high school level and have since returned to my alma mater, Yale, to earn my doctorate in American history. My thesis is on the Oregon Trail.
>
> I am single, healthy, and capable of pulling my own weight. I feel my presence could only benefit the passengers on your wagon train. I have chosen Professor

Harold Billings as a traveling companion. I think I would feel more comfortable having a colleague along who could discuss the historical importance of the sights we shall see. I'm most anxious to hear your views on Manifest Destiny when we meet.

Sincerely,
Johanna Remington

Freddy smiled to himself as he reread the last paragraph. Johanna Remington's words could be interpreted a number of ways. Whatever her meaning, she was a good candidate. Her history background would make her a valuable member of the expedition. Although she might be an intellectual snob, it wouldn't hurt to have a schoolmarm-type like Johanna along for the ride.

"You're still up?" a sleepy female voice asked from the darkened hallway beyond the living room. "I heard you groaning and talking to yourself. Is everything all right?"

"Watch your step," Freddy warned, reaching over to switch on an extra lamp. He held his hand out to his sister. "I've been reading the letters again and having last-minute thoughts about who should be included on the first trip. It's important that the gestalt of each group be—"

"Gestalt-schmalt. Save the fancy words for your fellow philosophy majors. Sounds like my favorite of the six Rotini brothers is badly in need of someone to talk to . . . in plain English." As she moved toward the sofa in her knee-length robe, Andee Rotini-Engborg's pregnant form seemed more pronounced.

Freddy chuckled softly at her rebuke, then opened his arms to welcome her against the protective warmth of his chest. "Thanks again for letting me stay here, borrow your mailbox, and disrupt your marriage while I suffer through this mid-life crisis."

"Mid-life?" Andee's tone held an echo of surprise. "You're barely thirty-three. And I keep telling you it's not a crisis. You're just a little nervous."

"I'm a long-haul truck driver attempting to pass myself off as a wagon master. I have good reason to be nervous. I'm no Boy Scout. I've never tried to light a campfire—or even look for kindling."

Freddy ran his fingers through his curly dark hair, then leaned his head back on the sofa. "Of all the damn luck. I'm afraid I share your talent for winning in Reno—"

"It must be genetic, Freddy. Isn't it wonderful?"

"Easy for you to say. You won *money.* I won an antique wagon train, a resentful crew, and a headache."

"Where's your sense of adventure? It's going to be fun." Andee nodded toward the piles of mail. "Now tell me about the people you chose to share this adventure with."

Freddy picked up several letters from the top of the five stacks and spread them in a row across the coffee table. "There're ten wagons," he began. "I wanted a good mix of families with children of varying ages, so I chose the Wongs, the Camerons, and the Prescotts."

"They're Chinese-American, black, and Caucasian, right?"

"Yeah, the kids will have a great time. They have a lot of mutual interests and common ages. And then there'll be a wagon of three single men and one of three single women."

"First you're a social engineer, now a match-maker?"

"I think it'll be interesting to see what happens," Freddy answered with a smile. "I've decided on the retired couple from California, and I'll put those three philosophy majors—one man and two women—in one wagon."

"Hmmm, are you sure that's such a great idea?" Andee frowned and folded her arms across her chest. "Forcing all those philosophers to live together for more than a week?"

"No one else could stand to be in close proximity with them for more than an hour, and they'll have a lot in common," Freddy said, brushing her concern aside. "Let's see—" he muttered as he pulled out the last of the letters. "There's this Johanna Remington and Professor Harold Billings—"

"The egghead history nuts. Miss Manifest Destiny and Humorless Harry. I can see it now."

"For a published and somewhat famous poet, you really have a way with words, Andee." Freddy shook his head. "Anyway, that leaves two wagons for the crew, Charlie, and myself."

"Poor Charlie."

"Would you stop referring to him as 'poor Charlie' all the time?"

"Well, he lost his livelihood in a poker game, and now he's working for you. That wagon train must have been in his family for years."

"He's a former used-car salesman who's been running the wagon trek for five years, Andee. And he still has a livelihood. I'm making him lead driver, paying him well, and letting him teach me the ropes."

"Poor Charlie." Andee sighed. "At least he has his longtime friends and fellow wranglers. The rest of the crew really sounds . . . interesting."

"They're fine if you like ads for after shave, jeans, and cigarettes. I only met them once but we're talking head-to-foot macho. And then there's the arrogant cook, James LaVish. The guy's a graduate of a little-known culinary institute, and he's two hundred and fifty pounds of frustrated chef. We had to totally rework his Cordon Bleu menu—"

"And he's poor Charlie Vishtek's son. Did James Vishtek change his name to James LaVish for professional reasons?"

"That's what I heard. Now would you please stop with the 'poor Charlie' routine?" Freddy tossed Johanna Remington's letter on the table. "The guy took a gamble and lost. You might have noticed this has been somewhat traumatic for me, as well. What about your brother—*poor Freddy?*"

"What's happened to our family philosopher lately?" Andee rested her hands on her rounded abdomen and looked up at her brother. "Why all the self-doubt?"

Feeling the weight of his sister's words, Freddy looked into Andee's large brown eyes, so like his own, and tried to smile. It was difficult.

"I just leased out the eighteen-wheeler I've been making payments on for ten years. I've placed ads in national magazines for a summer of wagon treks I don't know the first thing about, and frankly, I'm jealous of you and Thor. Your lives seem so . . . stable—compared to mine."

It was true. Spending time with Andee and her husband had made Freddy feel dissatisfied.

"Come on. You're not being fair. Our life is far from perfect, Freddy." Andee stifled a yawn that gave testimony to the late hour. "Besides, you never could stand to stay in one place too long."

"The urge to settle down with one person is growing stronger, Andee, but it would have to be a person who could understand my gypsy soul." Freddy shook his head. "Now I'm going from eighteen wheels back down to four, give or take a few pairs of horses or mules."

Freddy looked through the expanse of living room windows at the hauntingly beautiful mountains that served as a backdrop to Taos, New Mexico. They were illuminated by a full moon in a cloudless sky. "I wish you and Thor could come along."

"Next year," Andee promised. "The baby will be a seasoned traveler by then. Maybe you'll have learned how to build a fire. In the meantime, can you do me a big favor?"

"What kind of favor?" Freddy asked warily.

"Take Poco along with you this summer. As I get bigger, I have trouble seeing him." She spread her palms over the crest of her expanding stomach. "I'm afraid I might step on him and do some permanent damage."

"Andee, don't you think that's a fairly weak reason to pawn that runt of a dog off on me for the summer?"

"It's a serious problem," she insisted. "He blends

in with the terrain around here. It's impossible to take him for a walk—did I mention that I'm teaching a series of poetry seminars? The first one is in Santa Fe while Thor is doing a photography assignment in Texas. I'd rather not keep Poco at the kennel."

"Why me? Don't you have neighbors?"

"Poco loves you. It might help if you gave him some special attention before he has to get used to sharing the limelight with the baby."

"Andee, you know how I feel about that Chihuahua. He's so—so *little*. Besides, what will people think of a wagon master who has a twelve-ounce dog sitting at his elbow? Face it. He's no Rin-Tin-Tin."

"He has a Rin-Tin-Tin heart," Andee argued.

"He looks like a toy with teeth," Freddy protested. "Don't misunderstand. I like dogs, but I prefer something more . . . substantial. And you've got him so spoiled."

"Oh, all right," Andee said with a catch in her voice. "Although I really hate to cancel all the seminars, stop work on the nursery, and risk stepping on Poco."

Freddy glanced down at his sister's pleading expression. They came from the same loving, chaotic family. Andee had been born five years after the last of the six brothers. Now, as adults, all six men found it impossible to deny her anything.

"Okay, okay, I'll do it," Freddy said reluctantly. "I book passage for the little runt—but he rides *inside* the crew wagon and stays out of sight, understand?"

Andee nodded. "You two will work it out," she said cheerfully.

But when Freddy turned his attention to Poco,

who entered the room as if on cue, the Chihuahua gave him a look that seemed almost smug.

It was going to be quite a trip, Freddy thought. With children, academics, cowboys, and a Chihuahua all living in close quarters, there should certainly be no dull moments on the ten-day trek.

CHAPTER ONE

JOHANNA REMINGTON LOOKED out the bus window at the flat prairie land and felt a wave of nostalgia for her childhood, a glorious innocence that had evolved into a painful, twisted memory that she had spent years trying to suppress. Those eighteen years of growing up in Missouri had seemed like a distant dream . . . until now.

She'd grown used to her sheltered existence within the walls of academia at Yale. There were few visual reminders of her life as a tomboy named "Joey" or the Missouri farmhouse where her parents had raised their only child. As the late-afternoon sun cast long shadows over the Nebraska scenery outside her bus window, forgotten memories, pleasant and painful, stirred within her.

But reality drifted back to her through the voice of Professor Harold Billings, seated beside her, reading aloud from a pioneer's diary of the Oregon Trail. "Johanna, don't you find this particular account of Scotts Bluff just fascinating?" he paused to ask.

Johanna glanced over at her bespectacled colleague. They'd be reaching the rendezvous site for the wagon train in a matter of minutes. With a flush of guilt, she realized for the first time what a terrible mistake she'd made. She didn't even like her traveling companion. It seemed the only thing they had in common was their love of history.

"Johanna, I asked you about Scotts Bluff—"

"Why don't we wait until we're on the trail to actually discuss anything remotely historical?" Johanna suggested. "I'm enjoying the scenery at the moment."

"Wouldn't you like to talk about the historical significance of this particular region?" Harold persisted.

"Not really," she answered with a smile. "There'll be time . . . later."

From her seat in the last row, Johanna studied her fellow passengers, all destined to ride with her for the next ten days. Everyone appeared to be in a state of fevered anticipation. It was contagious. She began to look forward to meeting wagon master Freddy Rotini. She pictured an old man with dark eyes squinting out of a leathery face, and a rotund body. An expert on the history of the Oregon Trail, he'd have vast storytelling abilities, a library of rare books, and a love for the pioneer lifestyle.

Freddy Rotini. This man would be a true profile in courage.

Freddy practiced his swagger behind one of the crew wagons. He knew the bus would arrive any moment, and he hadn't mastered the rolling strut that everyone in the crew seemed to have been born with. He had assumed the stiff leather in his new cowboy boots would instantly put more macho into his gait.

"Damn," he muttered. "I'm tempted to—"

Poco barked from inside the wagon. Instantly, the horses hitched on the edge of the camp reacted.

"Poco, you're going to have to put a cork in it," Freddy said, reaching inside the wagon and picking up the Chihuahua. "Every time you bark, you upset the livestock."

The small dog burrowed his nose inside Freddy's shirt and whimpered. "Andee spoils you too much. You're used to being held all the time and sung to. I have bad news for you, buddy. I am not going to sing that ridiculous song for you. You'll have to be satisfied with the cassette. No more live performances from this dude, understand?"

Poco stuck his head farther inside Freddy's shirt just as the bus pulled up. Anxious to meet the arrivals, Freddy stepped out into the clearing.

Within minutes, no less than ten children were running excitedly from wagon to wagon. The adults filed out of the bus as the crew lined up alongside Charlie and Freddy for the first formal introduction to their guests.

Freddy glanced down at Charlie's weathered face, beard, and leather vest. "Why don't you make the introductions?" he whispered to the former owner of the wagon train.

Charlie squinted up at him, his dark eyes twinkling with mischief. "You're the wagon master now, Mr. Rotini. It's your job to make the folks feel welcome. I'll just stand back and enjoy watchin'."

Poor Charlie. Freddy found himself using his sister's familiar refrain. *The old guy's probably torn up inside, and he's trying to be jocular*. Freddy stopped himself from stoking his guilt by swaggering over to the gathering of would-be pioneers and motioning his crew to follow.

The single men and women seemed young. Very young. Friendships were being developed at a much faster rate than Freddy had anticipated. The retired couple from California reached out to stroke Poco's head, making Freddy aware for the first time that the Chihuahua was still in his arms. The philosophy majors were already arguing over the meaning of the number of spokes in a wagon wheel. The three couples with children were looking over their shoulders nervously as the kids began interrogating the crew about how all of the equipment worked . . . after their fingers had touched everything.

Freddy extended his hand to the tall gangly fellow in the dark suit and tie. This had to be Humorless Harry, Freddy thought as he introduced himself.

"So you're the wagon master. I'm Professor Harold Billings." The scholarly gentleman rocked back on his heels and tapped his fingers on a dog-eared book. "Mr. Rotini, did you know that there's an average of one dead person every eighty yards along the Oregon Trail? Every *eighty* yards!"

Freddy swallowed hard. He was speechless for a moment. "Every eighty yards, you say?" He watched as the professor nodded. "Well, let's not mention it to the others until after everyone's eaten, Harold. It's not exactly dinner conversation."

Freddy turned toward the last person to leave the bus. It had to be Miss Manifest Destiny—Johanna

Remington. He couldn't see her face because her back was turned toward him as she attempted to tie the strings on a sleeping bag. The slippery fabric was unraveling on the ground as she intensified her efforts.

He had expected a dumpy schoolmarm in a cotton dress and sensible shoes. *Too many* Wagon Train *reruns,* he told himself. *It just goes to show you how television uses and abuses stereotypes.*

Miss Manifest Destiny was a slender, modern-day schoolmarm-type instead, wearing fresh-off-the-rack indigo blue jeans and a tailored red shirt. Her dark hair was knotted at the nape of her neck. There had been a certain haughty quality in her letter and application form, he recalled. Freddy smiled. It would be hard for her to maintain that superior attitude bent over on her knees fighting an uncooperative sleeping bag and losing the battle.

Freddy quickly stuffed Poco deep inside his shirt and knelt on the grass beside her. "You must be Johanna Remington. Can I help you?" he offered.

"The nerve!" she sputtered.

"I just wanted to—"

"No, not you. I'm talking about Harold." Johanna didn't bother to look up at the man addressing her. She was too angry and frustrated. "My traveling companion got the strings of his sleeping bag caught on the bus door, dropped this mess at the foot of the steps, and waltzed off in search of some poor innocent soul to bore to death."

"Speaking of death"—Freddy tried to lighten the mood of the conversation"—Harold mentioned some rather ghoulish statistics about the number of—"

"You have my sympathy. I know exactly what

you're going to say. *You,* poor man, were his first victim." Johanna stopped struggling with the slippery fabric and looked up for the first time—into the warm brown eyes and captivating smile of a dark-haired stranger. "You must be a member of the crew," she stammered. "You weren't on the bus."

"I'm Freddy Rotini—"

"The wagon master?" Johanna stared in disbelief. Then her eyes drifted downward. The moist brown nose of some kind of animal poked out from between the buttons of his shirt.

Had he caught their dinner and stowed it in his shirt for safekeeping with the intention of killing it later? She recalled the brochure. It had mentioned some sort of stew. Her stomach churned with pity for the wild thing. "I think there's something moving inside your shirt," she said quietly.

Freddy wanted to tell her it was his heart. But it couldn't be, because his heart seemed to have stopped beating at the sight of her beautiful features and intense gray eyes, whose luminous quality competed with the large pearl earrings shimmering beside the ebony silk of her hair.

A strand had come undone from her austere hairstyle and lay across one high cheekbone. There was something sensuous about the way it hung loose and free so close to the edge of her mouth, fluttering slightly with each breath she took.

Her soft mouth was parted in surprise. She was wearing lipstick—a bright red shade that matched the scarlet hue of her tailored shirt. He saw her eyes flicker from his face back down to the center of his shirt.

Reaching up, Freddy slowly worked the buttons

free. Johanna watched as the smooth tanned expanse of his upper chest was exposed. She felt a sudden intimacy pass between them. They were both kneeling on the grass beside a rumpled sleeping bag and this youthful wagon master seemed to be in the process of taking off his shirt.

As she was about to protest, the last button slipped from its buttonhole to reveal a fawn-colored Chihuahua with huge mournful eyes. It whined pitifully and offered her a paw.

"Oh, thank God!" she said, suppressing a laugh. "I thought you were holding our dinner in your shirt."

"Our dinner?" Freddy was puzzled.

"I didn't know what you made the stew from," Johanna confessed.

"There's a choice of chicken, beef, or rabbit," Freddy said in an attempt to reassure her. He pulled Poco from his hiding place and nestled the dog casually against his chest.

Johanna stared at the man and dog for a second before returning to her struggle with the sleeping bag. She had expected a wagon master with white whiskers and a weatherbeaten brow. Freddy Rotini was a bronzed Adonis with riveting brown eyes. The man's western wear seemed as new as hers, and he couldn't be over thirty-five. As a rule, she tried to avoid judging people too quickly, but this wagon master seemed to have a thing about small dogs. What kind of harebrained outfit had she signed up with?

"I offered to help," Freddy reminded her.

"That's all right, you seem to have your hands full . . . of fur," Johanna said tersely.

Embarrassed, Freddy set Poco down on the grass

and pulled a rubber squeak toy out of his shirt pocket. He placed the toy hamburger beside the dog before he grabbed the end of the sleeping bag. "I know it looks silly—the Chihuahua and all—but my sister is pregnant, and I have to baby-sit the little beast while Andee gives poetry seminars. She's gotten Poco rather spoiled, as you've probably noticed."

"Hmmm, I've noticed." She sat back on her heels.

"You like animals, Johanna?" Freddy asked as he tied the strings of the sleeping bag firmly together.

Once again, she felt captured in the web of past memories. "I guess so—well, I used to." Johanna smoothed her hair back as she rose to her feet and moved away from him. Retreat from intimacy had always been the best remedy for her pain.

Freddy looked up into her face in time to catch a wistful shadow cross her finely chiseled features. "You're not sure?"

"I didn't say I loathe lower forms of life," Johanna countered. Why were they having this conversation? She felt an urge to run back to her ivy-covered university and lose herself in a stack of books. Dealing with the outside world could be so . . . exhausting. "Let's just say that there was a time when I was crazy about anything on four legs and now—" She searched for an explanation. "I'm involved in more serious endeavors," she said finally.

Freddy wanted to ask how she felt about male animals who walked on two legs but held his tongue. He sensed that Johanna had been struggling with something larger than a sleeping bag when he'd encountered her five minutes ago beside the bus.

The bus driver finished unloading the gear from

the lower compartments, and guests gathered around to claim and organize their belongings.

Freddy watched the chaotic scene for a moment, then turned back to Johanna. "Oh, I almost forgot. You'll be wanting to know about your wagon assignment." He spoke in a cheerful tone as he pulled a list from his pocket. "You're in . . . number ten. You and Professor Billings will be in the same wagon throughout the trip, but we'll switch positions every day so no one gets an unfair amount of dust." He stood up, carefully avoiding Poco, and grabbed the troublesome sleeping bag. She was standing a few feet from him, surveying the gathering of guests. For a moment, Freddy was surprised by her height. She was tall. Very tall. As she began to walk toward the piles of gear, he noticed the practiced elegance with which she carried herself.

After picking up Poco with his free arm, he caught up to her side with a few swift strides. "Will the professor be sleeping inside the wagon with you or on the ground?" he asked, nodding to indicate the sleeping bag under his arm.

"On the ground." Johanna made her reply firmly. The question was somewhat personal, and she felt uncomfortable under the scrutiny of Freddy's sensuous dark eyes. This man made her feel as though he could read her thoughts.

"I'm a very private person, Mr. Rotini." It was a simple statement, but she uttered each word with quiet insistence, and Freddy detected a steely warning in her voice.

He had felt like an intruder in the camp for the past two days, a stranger eating and sleeping beside men who had experienced this journey together before. For a moment, he had hoped that Johanna, a fellow outsider, could become a friend to him. As she told him that she was a "private person," he felt a door being shut in his face.

"I understand," Freddy said simply. He lowered Harold's sleeping bag slowly to the ground and walked past Johanna to attend to his other guests.

"For the next ten days, you'll catch a glimpse of the past and challenge yourselves much as the early pioneers did." Freddy shoved his hands deep into the pockets of his jeans. He glanced at the anxious faces that formed a circle around the campfire, pausing for a moment when his eyes met Johanna's.

Miss Manifest Destiny sat apart from the others, her hands wrapped protectively around her knees. Humorless Harry had eaten his meal with the talkative trio of philosophers. Freddy gave Johanna a second fleeting glance before continuing with his introductory speech.

"You'll watch some beautiful sunrises and eat hearty breakfasts from our chuck wagon. After the gear is packed up and the teams hitched, you'll travel throughout the day, but there'll be plenty of time to ride horses, swim, hike, fish, and relax."

Freddy looked down at his new boots. He made a small circle in the dirt with one toe as he spoke to the assembly of crew and guests. "You'll stop for lunch, and of course, we can halt anytime the scenery is breathtaking."

As he briefly described the historic sites along the trail, he studied the faces in the crowd. The group of singles had already paired into three couples by the time supper had been served an hour earlier. Families drew close, and even Harold had found his niche among the group from the philosophers' wagon. In fact, everywhere he glanced, people seemed to be sharing the warmth of the flickering firelight. Except of course, Johanna.

"Each evening after supper, there'll be singing or square dancing, and storytelling. We plan to have a talent night, so start planning your acts now." He felt his own enthusiasm bubble up in his voice. "You can always take time to sit beneath the prairie moon and think about the folks who passed this way more than a century ago."

Freddy smiled. He'd dreaded this speech for days, but the group was responding with happy, animated faces. "I hope that when our journey ends, we'll all feel like we belong to one big family. Any questions?"

"Mr. Rotini, can wild animals get inside the camp?" one of the younger children stood up and asked, her brow furrowed beyond her years.

Freddy put a hand over his mouth to hide his smile. The small girl's fingers were turning her father's arm white. *Too much television,* he thought. But as he glanced at the faces of the adults, he saw equal concern in some of their expressions.

"What's your name?" he asked, noting that the child sat on the bench next to Johanna's.

"Tiffany . . . with two little *f*s."

"We'll be perfectly safe, Tiffany-with-two-little-*f*s," he assured the youngster and those who shared her concern. "We're only playing at being pioneers on this trip. Sometimes playing is more fun if you pretend it's more dangerous than it is—"

Johanna leaned forward and rested her chin on

one of her upraised knees. She liked the way Freddy was interacting with the frightened child. Perhaps this wagon master wasn't the profile in courage she had expected, but he had a sense of humor and a heart. And he looked wonderful in firelight.

Suddenly, she sat up and folded her arms across her chest. This was ridiculous. Freddy Rotini wouldn't be of any help to her on this trip unless he proved himself an expert in her area of interest. She couldn't let his hypnotic voice and firelit features sway her opinion of him. She had to think of him as a resource . . . for her life's work.

"You see, years ago there *were* dangers on the Oregon Trail, but you don't have to worry because the crew is here to make sure things are always safe." Freddy's eyes never left Tiffany's as he sat down on one of the rustic log benches surrounding the fire. He was suddenly grateful for the books on the Oregon Trail that his sister Andee had thoughtfully purchased for him before the trip.

"More than one hundred years ago, there were untamed areas of wilderness all along the trail." As he spoke, Freddy gestured with the abandon that was typical of his family. He cast an eyes in Charlie Vishtek's direction. Charlie was a master storyteller. Freddy decided he would simply lead into an introduction that would allow the former wagon master's talents to be showcased.

"There were cougars and bears and the mighty buffalo." Freddy pronounced each word breathlessly, inwardly cursing his own wild imagination. Pictures of these wild beasts filled his mind. Beyond the comforting glow of the campfire, shadows flickered against the white canvas sides of the surrounding wagons. He swallowed hard. "And of course, there were wolves and coyotes—"

"Yip, yip, yip." Without warning, a small ball of fur, fangs bared, jumped into his lap and scrambled up the front of his shirt toward his neck. Startled, Freddy fell over backward on the bench with a yelp.

The crowd drew a communal intake of breath that turned to laughter as Freddy righted himself, grasping Poco the Chihuahua in one hand.

"Bad boy! Didn't I tell you to stay in the wagon?" Freddy hissed under his breath as the laughter died.

Johanna smiled as the wagon master, with a sheepish grin, took the rubber hamburger out of his shirt pocket and gave it to the small dog. So, Freddy could laugh at himself and could bear to be laughed at. There were things about him that made it easy to like this man—from a safe distance.

Rising, his cheeks still stained red with embarrassment, Freddy crossed over to the bench where the little girl sat. He held out the source of his confusion.

"You see, Tiffany, we have nothing to fear. This wagon train has a specially trained attack dog that not only warns us if wild animals are around but lectures anyone who dares to *describe* such creatures. This is Poco."

As he spoke, Freddy's eyes shifted over to the next bench and met Johanna's. For a brief moment, she returned his smile. After handing Poco to Tiffany, he gathered his courage and sat in the vacant spot beside Johanna. He watched her back straighten and felt her retreat behind some invisible barrier when his knee brushed hers.

Setting this two-person drama aside, he returned his attention to his duties as wagon master. In a loud voice, he told the crowd he was turning the storytelling over to an expert, and gave Charlie a flamboyant introduction.

Johanna applauded with the others but sat frozen to the bench. In almost thirty years of living, she had loved only one man, Ronnie Buck Ferguson. With his dark curly hair and intense brown eyes, Freddy Rotini not only resembled Ronnie Buck, he shared the same haunting laugh and the ability to show a very human vulnerability. It was that vulnerability that frightened Johanna.

Perhaps she'd fled to the East Coast and surrounded herself with flawless male statues—men who were not quite real enough for her—for that reason. She'd learned about love from Ronnie Buck as a young woman, and she'd gloried in the depth of her emotions. But in the end, she'd come away remembering only pain. Searing, unforgettable pain.

The Nebraska scenery, the campfire, the hearty stew supper, and her meeting with Freddy Rotini had combined to make this a day for remembering. *Her childhood*. Her love of the midwestern scenery. Her initiation into the mysteries of womanhood. How did a person separate the warm, loving memories from the harsh, unforgiving kind?

She looked down at Freddy's boots. They were too new. There were things about this man that didn't fit the image of an experienced wagon master. At moments, he seemed out-of-place, and yet his self-deprecating humor endeared him to those gathered around the campfire. While an inner voice warned her to avoid the chance of another painful encounter, her curiosity plagued her with questions that begged to be answered. And the scholar in her was rapidly accumulating questions of another sort—about his background. What qualified him to lead this venture?

Freddy waited patiently throughout the tall tale that Charlie spun. When one of the cowboys pulled out a harmonica and another produced a guitar, he used the quiet interlude to turn to Johanna. She must have anticipated his movement, he thought. She was turned in his direction, her face full of firelight, her large gray eyes questioning.

"There's going to be a square dance tomorrow night," he said quietly. "I'd appreciate it if you'd save a dance for me, Johanna."

She looked into the fire as she answered. "I'd think a wagon master would have his hands full with a myriad of responsibilities. Do you have time to enjoy dancing with all the women, or do you feel sorry for me because I'm sitting alone, Mr. Rotini?"

Freddy rested his hands on his knees, stared at the ground for a moment, then responded matter-of-factly. "You shoot straight from the hip, don't you, Ms. Remington?"

"Yes, I do." Johanna nodded. "As a rule."

"All right. First of all, forget the formalities. The name is Freddy. Second, pity is not even close to the way I'd describe the feelings I have about you. And last of all"—he reached out with his fingertips and turned her head to face him squarely— "I want to dance with you tomorrow night because I love these prairie stars and I want to see them reflected in your eyes. Does that answer your question?"

There was a pause. People were humming along to the harmonica and guitar. The communal hum seemed to vibrate incessantly against Johanna's backbone. She felt herself relax.

"Please, call me Joey." *Joey*. The nickname that connected Johanna to her childhood, to Ronnie Buck Ferguson, and to all that she wished to forget, was out before she could stop herself.

CHAPTER TWO

FREDDY LAY ON TOP of his sleeping bag on the hard ground and stared up at the stars. Most of the crew members were bedding down outside tonight. He envied the easy camaraderie they shared. Turning his head, he watched the youngest wrangler pass a cup of coffee along to one of the seasoned drivers, his boyish eyes shining with respect.

The group talked about horses and mules, harnesses and knots, tomorrow's terrain, and the weather. The weather was the only thing Freddy felt qualified to discuss unless someone was inclined to mention long-haul trucking or philosophy. And there was his problem with the "drawl."

He had almost mastered the swagger. Now he found himself memorizing the colorful phrases the crew used to describe everyday events. Freddy wished at times that he had purchased an "Oregon Trail/English" phrase book to assist him in understanding the crew. But the most important language, the universal language of helping the guests feel welcome and at home, was shared by all of them and well understood.

As the conversation lulled, the men lowered their voices and turned to more earthy matters: the womenfolk. Every female on the journey was evaluated and cataloged. Freddy frowned, waiting for their appraisal of Johanna Remington. He had never enjoyed locker-room talk. It bothered him even more as he gazed up at the stars and thought of Johanna's large gray eyes and the unexpected request to call her "Joey."

"What'ya think of the prissy miss in the red shirt?" a lanky mule skinner, leaning against one of the wagons, asked a comrade.

"She jus' needs a good man t' teach her how to relax a little."

As suggestions were made as to how each man would achieve such a transformation, Freddy squirmed. He had met Johanna just that afternoon, yet he felt protective. Besides, he hated to see any woman discussed like chattel. Poco whined and pawed Freddy's forearm.

"What is it, boy? Have to use the facilities?"

He didn't know why he bothered to ask a dog such a question. He was risking his newly acquired status as wagon master, and Poco wasn't about to give him an intelligent answer in English. He had heard his sister talking to Poco so often that it had become a habit to address the dog like a human. A very small human.

"Go ahead," Freddy urged as he pushed the Chihuahua toward the darkened area beyond the camp. "Don't be afraid, boy. Go by yourself."

Poco whined until Freddy got up and walked him to the riverbank. When they returned to the camp, the other crew members were turning in for the night. Freddy climbed inside his sleeping bag, acutely aware of the strain the events of the day had incurred on his body and mind.

Poco put a small paw over Freddy's mouth, the signal that he wanted to be sung to.

"No."

The dog was insistent. Freddy was sure his lip must be bleeding from the last onslaught of canine toenails.

"Come here," he hissed, stuffing the small dog inside the sleeping bag. He was prepared for this. The crew had snickered the last two nights, first when he had tried to sing the song, and then again when he had played it on his small stereo.

Freddy took out a tiny cassette unit, adjusted the volume for a moment, then put a pair of headphones over the dog's large ears. Poco's eyes lit up with gratitude.

"You're spoiled to the bone," Freddy muttered as he glanced around. No one had heard or seen a thing this time. He smoothed Poco's back for a moment, listening to the muted sound of his sister Andee singing her pet's favorite lullaby over and over until soon both man and dog were asleep.

Johanna paused on the climb up Windlass Hill and felt breathless—not from the exertion of the hike but from the sight of the celebrated wagon ruts to her left, leading down from the stone monument atop the hill. So many emigrants had made references to this dangerous landmark in their diaries. "Just imagine—"

"Imagine what?" Harold looked up from the stack of books and maps he juggled in his arms.

She ignored his dour expression. "Look at the jagged scars left by the wagons. *This* is the Oregon Trail, Harold. It's not in those books you're holding. It's here—beneath our feet!"

Her companion glanced briefly up at the monument, then down at the eroded ground. "I'm anxious to see the library at Bridgeport," he mumbled.

"That's all you've talked about," Johanna exclaimed with a sigh.

"I believe it's the most extensive collection of books on the Oregon Trail in existence."

"Well, we're not in Bridgeport yet, Harold," Johanna reminded him as they neared the top of the hill where other members of the wagon train were standing. "We're at Windlass Hill and about to get our first glimpse of Ash Hollow. Look at how the wagon ruts are getting deeper—from erosion, I would guess."

At the crest, she took a deep breath and understood why so many fellow passengers were rooted to the spot. The view was breathtaking. "That's where we'll camp tonight, Harold." She shook his arm. "See the swale of the wagon ruts? Don't you find it a monument to hope, to the strength of the human spirit? It's incredibly—"

"*Distracting and time-consuming,*" Harold finished. "I can't wait to get to the library."

Johanna ignored her wagon mate's muttering. She recalled the journal entries concerning this spot and felt overwhelmed with empathy for the travelers who had struggled on the trail's first steep descent, all to start a new life.

Harold's sharp tone intruded on her thoughts.

"I don't see why we have to stop for every two-bit monument and grave along the road. We're going to miss the important things! For a doctoral student, you don't seem to be sharing my enthusiasm for the true historical ramifications of this journey. That library is a gold mine. If you expect to get your thesis published—"

Johanna was becoming increasingly impatient with Harold's harping tone. Other members of the wagon train meandered nearby, talking excitedly about the view and looking through guidebooks. She stopped to talk to a small child who had stumbled.

"You're not listening, Johanna. I said I expect to peruse those volumes for several hours, if not more."

She smiled at the youngster and touched his shoulder as he started off in the direction of his parents. "Maybe Freddy will be kind enough to let you borrow the crew's Jeep when we're close to Bridgeport so you can spend more time in town—"

"So Mr. Rotini has become Freddy now."

"A lot of people on the train call him Freddy."

"I don't have to like it, you know," Harold muttered, pouting. "That man doesn't have a serious bone in his body."

Johanna shaded her eyes from the afternoon sun and squinted at the inscription on the monument. Harold was right, of course. She didn't know why she felt inclined to defend Freddy. "How can you make a judgment like that after so little time?" she asked beneath her breath.

"This Freddy person hasn't answered one of my questions about the Oregon Trail in the dignified manner I expected of an established wagon master."

"Well, not all of his guests are history professors. Maybe he wants the trip to be . . . fun," Johanna countered. She turned from her companion and began walking down the trail.

"Fun?" Harold's strangled cry echoed in her ears.

Freddy glanced in the small mirror that hung on the side of the crew wagon. Without a hairdryer, his curly hair turned mutinous. One dark lock refused to be tamed and hung over his forehead in a defiant wave.

Sighing, he stepped back, adjusted a nearby lantern, and tried to catch a glimpse of the shirt he had just put on. It was white and cut in a western style. There was a line of fringe over the chest, across the back, and along the arms. He had purchased it for special occasions, and tonight's square dance fit that description. He fingered the smooth border, letting the satiny strands slide through his fingertips as he tried to get a clear view in the mirror. He had to settle for seeing only a portion of his anatomy at a time.

Satisfied, Freddy glanced under the wagon where Poco was tethered securely to the wheel. The Chihuahua was lying with his feet in the air, surrounded by squeeze toys, next to a mound of dog biscuits. He appeared to be playing "dead" and doing a rather convincing job of it.

"Go ahead and sulk," Freddy whispered. "For the last time, you're not going to the square dance. You're a dog."

Poco opened his eyes, rolled them back, and seemed to sigh audibly at this news.

Freddy walked toward the campfire as the opening strains of fiddle music filled the sweet night air. Small groups of people were gathering. The children talked excitedly and took turns demonstrating bone-breaking dance moves to an enraptured audience of adults.

Johanna stepped out of the shadows into the soft glow of the fire. Freddy exhaled at the sight of her. A white peasant blouse contrasted alluringly with the natural olive tint of her skin. His eyes were drawn to the soft thrust of her breasts against the fabric, then moved downward to the red woven sash at the waist of her jeans. Her hair was pulled back loosely in a long ponytail. Wisps of dark hair curled about her face, framing her features and softening the shy smile she gave him when their eyes met.

Harold Billings, dressed in a black western shirt with silver piping, walked up behind her and spoke into her ear. Freddy watched the interlude with interest. Why would a woman consent to travel for ten days with a man she so openly disliked? Or was that a subjective perception?

Charlie stood up on a small makeshift platform and gave a short informal explanation of the easiest square dance calls. Then the musicians broke loose, and Freddy's social engineering experiment proved successful. Couples, some of them newly formed, laughed nervously as they attempted the moves. Children of all ages formed their own circle and added a youthful flair to the standard calls.

Freddy began to move toward Johanna's side, but Harold had already placed an arm around her waist.

Freddy had to smile. Was this to be a hoedown or a showdown? Johanna had promised him a dance and he'd demand it, he told himself, before the night was through.

Johanna glanced across the camp at the broad-shouldered wagon master, whose eyes seemed to follow her every move. This was insane. He looked like something out of a Wild West sideshow. She hadn't had a chance to ask him any questions about his background; he could be a slick huckster. She was an intelligent woman, and yet, she felt drawn to him.

As the dance drew to a close, she thanked Harold curtly and walked purposefully toward Freddy. He met her halfway, where the firelight was most intense.

"You remembered your promise." Freddy's warm velvet voice sent a shudder through her, and the feel of his fingers on the small of her back made her tilt her face upward. "Your unspoken promise," he added, glancing at the night sky. "And the stars seem to be cooperating for us. Your eyes are already beginning to reflect them."

"Mr. Rotini—" she protested, taken aback by his flowery speech.

Ignoring her words, he laced the fingers of his right hand through hers and stared up at Charlie for instructions.

She felt the cool fringe of his shirt swirl against her bare arms as they promenaded and did do-si-dos for the next five minutes, moving about the circle of dancers yet always finding each other and smiling as their fingers touched.

This is foolish, Johanna thought. They'd hardly spoken to each other except at short intervals last night and throughout this first day on the road. She was acting like a schoolgirl, overcome with strong feelings of attraction for this mystery man in white fringe with the defiant curl hanging over his forehead. She expected him at any moment to pull on a mask, throw her a silver bullet, and disappear into the darkness.

Wasn't that the way her love affair with Ronnie Buck had ended? In a trail of dust as he announced his engagement to a college sweetheart in Texas? She wanted to withdraw as the pain of the long-forgotten memory seemed to echo in the plaintive cry of the cowboy's fiddle. Then Freddy's laughter drew her back.

He had the most marvelous laugh. Johanna found it hard not to smile at the sound of his deep-throated chuckle. If a voice could produce a feeling of déjà vu, then Freddy's laughter seemed to resonate from a past life—or a life she wished she'd shared with him.

After two fast-moving tunes, the musicians gave the breathless dancers a break. Couples sought each other out for a slow dance. Johanna felt Freddy's arms move around her wordlessly, and she welcomed his embrace.

"Does everyone call you Joey?" he asked quietly when the music started.

Johanna almost choked. It was the first time he had spoken her nickname in that rich magical voice of his. She was the one who was vulnerable now.

"Actually, no one has called me that for about ten years," she answered after a moment's pause. "It started when I was a tomboy in Missouri. I was an only child and my family had a farm in the Ozark

Mountains, so it was natural for me to grow up enjoying the outdoors."

"I've always found myself attracted to women from the Midwest. There's something very honest, yet warm and loving about them, don't you think?"

She felt it happening, felt herself retreating from his intimacy. "I wouldn't know." Johanna's words were hesitant. This man had a way of saying things that threw her off. She was never at a loss for words in the academic world, but here, under this big Nebraska sky, she was speechless. "I've spent so much of my time in the East these past ten years, that I haven't given it much thought. Geographically, I don't see why that phenomenon would occur. I doubt that anyone's compiled the necessary data—"

"No words over four syllables for the next hour, please."

She looked up just as Freddy winked and gave her a dizzying swirl. The stars blurred for a brief second as the smooth fringe on his shirt sleeve swayed against her bare forearm. She found herself staring into her partner's unblinking brown eyes.

"Do you have something against intelligent conversation, Freddy?" Johanna asked as she raised an eyebrow.

"I love it—in the right places and at the right times. But this isn't the place or time. I want to know more about Johanna Remington, the person. We'll talk about Manifest Destiny and collect necessary data another time."

Johanna remembered her letter, and stifled the laugh that had gathered in her throat.

Regaining her composure, she said, "I'm afraid I'm not very interesting—"

"Former tomboys are always interesting. Sometime during the next ten days, we'll have to climb trees, hunt snakes, go fishing, and . . . build a fort together."

His comments stopped her again. There seemed to be a double meaning to his last suggestion. "Keeping up with this wagon train is going to be enough of an adventure for me, thank you," Johanna said with a smile. "My companion isn't much help. He'd rather read than tackle the assigned chores."

"Oh, I don't know. Harold seems like a . . . nice enough fellow." Freddy glanced over at the tall, thin man dressed in black, who was glaring at the two of them from the edge of the circle of dancers. "He does appear a bit possessive at times, though."

"I think he has a romantic interest in me that he's never really expressed before." Johanna shook her head. "Either that, or I've been too busy to notice it."

Freddy rested his cheek against her temple. "If I expressed a romantic interest in you, Ms. Remington, I doubt you'd be too busy to notice."

The sudden compulsion to kiss her was overwhelming. Dancing away from the firelight and into the shadows, he used the cover of darkness to touch his lips to the high arch of her cheek. She tensed but didn't draw back as he had expected. "Do I have your attention now?" he asked in a husky whisper.

Johanna gave him her full attention. She wouldn't play these foolish games. It was time to ask the man a pointed question.

"Do you remember what I said?" He spoke before she could challenge his credentials.

"Uhhh," she stammered. Had her mind turned to mush? "No four-letter words, and we'll build a fort."

"Almost," Freddy said with a chuckle. "No four-syllable words. And you're right... about the fort ... Joey."

Johanna wrapped a long strand of her dark hair around her hand and sighed. Her legs and bare feet were lost in the tall grass where she sat. Unable to sleep, she had walked toward the bank of the stream to think. The experience of square dancing with Freddy was still swirling through her mind. At the end of the evening, he had touched her shoulder gently before turning to his chores as wagon master and listing the next day's events for his guests.

She could only compare herself to a naive freshman in awe of an upperclassman. But the comparison didn't work. She wasn't in awe of Freddy. Throughout her adult life, she had towered over men literally because of her height, and often figuratively because of her intellect, as well. She wasn't used to playing the simpering female at a loss for words.

That made the intensity of her attraction for Freddy hard to understand. "Build a fort together?" Come on. If this romantic diversion continued, she'd lose sight of the purpose of her journey, and then where would she be?

Perhaps she'd had her head in history books too long and was finally coming up for air. The campus was swarming with handsome males who looked as though they walked out of the slick pages of a men's fashion magazine. She'd never dreamed that white fringe and an unruly curl would turn her head.

The wind rustled through the elm trees overhead,

and she vowed to herself that tomorrow she would quit daydreaming about an impossible match and try to become more amicable toward Harold Billings. He was a man of letters, and he had integrity.

But Harold didn't talk about stars reflecting in her eyes or brush warm lips against her cheek.

At that moment, a deep male voice caught her attention. Someone was walking nearby. And something else was whining. It could mean only one thing.

"Use the facilities like a good boy and we'll call it a night."

Freddy was talking, or rather pleading, with *that dog*. Johanna felt she was eavesdropping, but it would be more embarrassing to stand up and attempt to join the "conversation." After several minutes of silence, Freddy spoke again.

"The crew hasn't exactly welcomed us with open arms, have they? Face it, boy. We're both impostors. You're a poor excuse for a dog, and I have no right to be called a wagon master."

Impostor? What was he talking about? Johanna wondered. She watched as Freddy, in silhouette, moved closer to the stream.

"You know what kills me?" Freddy asked the dog. Poco whined in responsc. "Seeing the light in poor Charlie's face grow dim when someone refers to me as the wagon master. Lord, it just tears me apart. Maybe he was drinking or emotionally upset the night I won the wagon train away from him in Reno. How can I live with the thought of that? I feel like a thief."

Freddy had won the wagon train gambling? Johanna was growing more confused. This was like listening to a stranger's private thoughts. But Freddy was no longer a stranger to her. He had held her close and whispered veiled innuendos in her ear while they danced. And he had occupied her thoughts throughout the day.

"I'm still trying to figure out the difference between a bullwhacker and a mule skinner," he continued. "I don't know that it matters, Poco, but it couldn't hurt my relationship with the crew if I understood their dialect."

Freddy bent over and picked up the dog. "And I'm cramming to learn something about the history of the area, but it looks stupid for a grown man to lie on his sleeping bag reading a book called *A Child's Introduction to the Oregon Trail*.

"What would Johanna think if she saw me curled up with *that* illustrious volume? I guess that'd be an impressive sight for someone studying for her doctorate on the subject. Of course, if she heard me carrying on one of these one-sided conversations with you, boy, she'd probably ask for a transfer to a bus heading east on the closest interstate."

Johanna frowned as she hugged her knees to her chest. It was Freddy's vulnerability that had drawn her to him in the beginning. It had been effective that first day, and it was even more potent now. Any man who could admit his weaknesses and attempt to correct them was very human.

But she couldn't allow herself to be attracted to a man because of his *human qualities*. Ronnie Buck had proven to her that it was also human to cheat and to lie. To hurt the person who loved you. No, she didn't need *human*, but she probably didn't need Harold, either. That was just her guilt speaking.

She sighed. Minutes earlier she'd been afraid of losing sight of the purpose of this journey. She had vowed to be more amicable toward Harold. Nice, safe Harold. *The purpose of this journey,* she reminded herself, *is to have fun—to get away from my work and take a vacation.*

Johanna knew the solution now. She would spend little time with either Harold *or* Freddy. She would do her chores, join in the social activities, and eat with the group, but she would remain aloof from the other members of the train.

Returning to the Midwest had brought questions to her mind that demanded answers. How much of that tomboy named Joey remained buried in her consciousness? From now on, she vowed anew, this would be a voyage of self-discovery no matter what the consequences. She would test her own strength and independence for the remainder of the journey. And in doing so, she'd find the answers to her questions.

"Johanna! Johanna Remington!"

"What is it now, Harold?" she said with a groan from beneath the wagon, where she was busy hanging a bucket of cream that she hoped would churn into butter by the end of the day.

"I refuse to share this wagon with you any longer!" Harold dropped to all fours to confront her face-to-face.

"Well, what's gotten into *you?*" Johanna scrambled from beneath the wagon's wooden bottom. "I've been up since five helping with breakfast and chores. I thought you were sleeping or reading—"

"I was reading." Harold pulled a small blue book

from under his suit jacket and waved it above his head. "I refuse to travel with a woman who is openly lusting after a mental midget!"

"Lusting? And what do you mean *mental midget*—" With a start, Johanna recognized the cover of her journal. "Oh, my God. You found my—"

"I just finished reading last night's entry." Harold held the book against his chest dramatically and fixed her with stony eyes. "I thought you were safe—your womanly warmth snuggled inside our wagon as I stood sentry patiently on the hard ground outside."

"I don't *snuggle*, and you weren't standing. You were sleeping—"

"That's even worse. I trusted you, and what do you do? You sneak off into the night and meet with your dubious white-shirted knight down by the water. How romantic."

"Harold, you're overreacting. Did you read the entire passage? Maybe I admitted to being attracted to the man, but later I mentioned that—" She stopped in mid-phrase. "Why am I trying to explain my life to you? You had no right to look through my belongings or read my journal."

Johanna flushed to think of the brief, hastily written entry she had made after returning from her midnight wanderings. It was obvious that Harold hadn't read the entire passage.

"I've packed my belongings, Ms. Remington," Harold sniffed, pointing to his overstuffed backpack and a rather lumpy sleeping bag, which was slowly unraveling at his feet. "I refuse to share a wagon with a woman of your easy virtue."

"Easy virtue? A woman can't lose her virtue sitting alone in three feet of grass in the dark, you overrated—!" Johanna hadn't lost her temper in years. Without realizing it, she picked up an empty pail and swung, only to meet a fierce resistance.

"Did someone mention easy virtue?" Freddy Rotini firmly held the sides of the uplifted pail. Gently, he eased it from her grip. "As wagon master, it's my duty to act as mediator if any disputes come up between people sharing the same wagon. It appears you two are going to be my first mediation."

"Oh, great. It's the mental midget come to save the day." Harold threw the blue journal to the ground in front of Johanna. "It won't help. My bags are packed. Do you have anything to say for yourself, Johanna?"

"Harold!" Johanna choked his name. She was still furious, and she didn't want Freddy to know the nature of this ridiculous argument. It was upsetting to think he had witnessed her loss of control and seen her pick up the pail. "I just want to know . . . where you're going to stay if you leave—"

"I'll travel with those three compassionate philosophers—if they'll have me. If not, I'll simply walk behind the wagon train, asking for water when thirsty, food when hungry, my bedroll when night falls . . ."

"Harold, cut the melodrama. This isn't a movie—yet." Johanna bent over and picked up her journal. "Admit it, you obtained information about me in a surreptitious manner."

"Speaking of surreptitious behavior"—Harold pointed a finger—"who appointed you the wagon train operative? Wait until I tell the head of the doctoral program his prize student was learning about the Oregon Trail by sneaking stealthily through the grasses to eavesdrop on—"

"You underhanded weasel," Johanna said in a fierce whisper.

"Harlot of the plains!" Harold shot back emphatically.

Freddy stepped between them, intrigued by the nature of the argument and shocked at the rapid deterioration of vocabulary. "How am I supposed to mediate if you two don't stop—"

It was too late. Harold stomped off toward the philosophers' wagon, leaving his possessions behind, and Johanna disappeared around the side of the wagon.

"What are you doing?" he asked her, circling the large vehicle. Freddy watched as Johanna grabbed a bowl of bread dough and began to knead it.

"I'm doing my assigned tasks before we start today's journey," she answered sharply, giving the dough a punch as if to emphasize her words.

Johanna was secretly relieved. She'd have the wagon to herself. She wouldn't have to worry about anyone interfering with her *voyage of self-discovery.*

"Aren't you concerned about traveling alone for the next nine days?" Freddy thought of the crude comments his crew had made concerning Johanna. She'd need a protector.

The warmth was gone from his voice. Johanna looked up and tried to put a name to the emotions that were passing over Freddy's features like fleeting clouds. Storm clouds.

"I'm quite capable of handling any . . . adventure that might befall us," Johanna assured him with a tilt of her chin. Harold's words still stung. *Lusting after a mental midget? Easy virtue? Harlot of the plains?* How dare he? She gave the dough another punch.

"There *are* dangers on the trail, Johanna." Freddy leaned against the wagon and pointed up at the sky. "You know, even a few fluffy little sheeplike clouds like those can turn into a howling tornado . . . in just minutes." He snapped his fingers for effect.

When she didn't seem impressed, he continued, "And of course, there are flash floods, thunderstorms, rattlesnakes, dust dervishes, forest fires, windstorms, and naturally, wild animals—to name a few of the minor dangers."

"I thought the camp had an attack dog for the express purpose of keeping wild animals away." Johanna lifted an eyebrow. Freddy's expression made her want to laugh. Had he learned about these dangers from *A Child's Introduction to the Oregon Trail* or from watching the weather station?

He was happy to see her interjecting humor into their conversation. Perhaps she was getting over her argument with Humorless Harry.

"You can't be too sure. Even attack dogs need a day off now and then. Say, you're kneading that dough pretty hard, aren't you?" he suggested in a good-natured tone.

"It's a family tradition. When we're upset, we take it out on our bread dough."

"I see." Freddy watched for a moment. He was anxious to learn about the subject of the argument but respected her privacy too much to ask. "Professor Billings said some unkind things. I take it you're still . . . upset?"

"In what capacity are you asking? As official mediator, curious bystander, or—"

"As a friend, Johanna," Freddy replied. He took the bowl out of her hands and set it inside the wagon. "And as of this moment, you won't have to do all of these chores alone. I'm going to be your new roommate."

"What?" She gave him an incredulous stare.

"No one—man or woman—travels alone in my wagon train. It's the rule. I know you have a dependable driver to handle your team during the day, but you need someone here in the evenings . . . and through the night." Freddy folded his arms across his chest. "I'll be that someone. You can trust me, Johanna."

"Oh, my God," she whispered beneath her breath. Last night she had vowed to test her own strength and independence no matter what the consequences. Freddy's constant presence was certainly going to put a kink in her plans. Johanna felt the heat rush to her face as she raised her eyes to meet the dark intensity of his gaze. "I think I'd rather chance the wild animals, Mr. Rotini."

Freddy chuckled and looked down at his boots. "You won't have to worry about wild animals. The attack beast will be traveling with us. I'll be back as soon as I grab my things . . . and Poco."

CHAPTER THREE

"YOU RIDE VERY WELL, Ms. Remington."

Thinking she was alone, Johanna started at the sound of a female voice. She turned in her saddle to find the source of the compliment and recognized the approaching black woman as one of the four occupants of the wagon positioned in front of hers. *The Cameron family.*

"Thank you, Mrs. Cameron. Please . . . call me Johanna."

"And I'd prefer being called Coni. It's nice to finally get a chance to talk to you." The attractive young woman tried to control her spirited mount. "I guess we'll be neighbors for the next week or so. First of all, please be honest and tell me if my kids kept you awake the past two nights. They were so excited about sleeping under the stars in their new superhero sleeping bags and matching pajamas."

"I didn't hear a thing," Johanna responded with a

smile. She didn't want to admit that she had spent much of her restless night down by the river.

"That surprises me." Coni widened her eyes. "Mercron the Meteoroid and Captain Orion came shrieking into our wagon at midnight. I think it was a case of too much excitement—the square dance and all. You like kids, Johanna?"

"Doesn't everyone? Actually, I was forced to when I taught high school history before starting work on my doctorate." Johanna slowed her pace. "I haven't spent much time around smaller kids, but whenever I do, I'm overwhelmed by a strange desire to take them home with me."

"That desire might dampen a little when you meet my two little space cowboys."

The sound of Coni's laughter was infectious and Johanna joined in.

"Coni," she said quietly. "Uh, I—I hope the *discussion* between Harold and myself this morning wasn't loud enough to disturb you."

"Don't worry." Coni Cameron gestured with her hand as if to brush Johanna's fears aside. "The wagon master paid us a visit, apologized for the disturbance, and explained that Professor Billings has moved out and he's moved in."

"Oh." Johanna was speechless. Coni made it sound so simple. Musical bunks. But there was nothing simple about having a man who was in the public eye, a man you were physically attracted to, a man you had resolved not to become romantically involved with, move his clothes and toiletries into your living space.

Johanna had watched helplessly that morning from a safe distance as Freddy brought two armloads of belongings and one small dog to her campsite. Then he'd had the nerve to whistle Beethoven's *Moonlight* Sonata as he arranged his bedroll and clothing in the space left by Harold's hasty departure. It rattled her, seeing Freddy's personal possessions so close to her own. Of course, she'd demand he sleep outside the wagon as her former companion had done, but they'd be forced to do chores together and interact no matter how much she objected.

Johanna had tried to escape the disturbing situation that morning by leaving her wagon in the capable hands of her assigned driver and taking to horseback. "Well, I suppose the wagon train is buzzing with the news that Freddy Rotini will be my new roommate."

"I don't think so," Coni said with a knowing glance. "I can't speak for the others, but we left the city and came on this trek to get away from the tension of our jobs. I'm not about to spend my vacation judging the actions of other people." Coni sighed. "Frankly, I think it's rather commendable that our Mr. Rotini feels so committed to the people on the train. He told my husband, Donald, and me that he refuses to let anyone travel alone. Now that's really gallant!"

Gallant? Johanna almost choked. How long would she have to wait to find out the real nature of his intentions?

The subject of Freddy Rotini was dropped as the two women continued riding, staying parallel with the slow-moving train of wagons but enjoying the freedom of their own meandering path.

Johanna discovered that Coni was the mother of a six-year-old and an eight-year-old son, was married to a professor of medieval history, and worked as an advertising salesperson for a television station in Atlanta. For an hour, their conversation drifted from work-related goals to the troubles of the world, then shifted to their private lives.

Johanna was forgetting her promise to remain aloof from other members of the train. She felt the warmth of a new friendship flickering into a small but brightly burning flame.

Coni was upbeat but down-to-earth, immersed in her marriage and family yet serious about her career in broadcast sales. In recent years, she'd suffered the death of her only sister and the diagnosis of her younger son's learning disabilities. The woman had an uncanny way of finding the bright side to every situation and interjecting humor into the mundane. Johanna wondered from what bottomless well Coni Cameron drew her cheerfulness.

"I had a feeling you and Professor Billings were simply colleagues when I first spotted the two of you on the bus," Coni confessed quietly. "Anyone in your life you're serious about?"

"No, not right now." Johanna rubbed her thumb against the polished leather of the reins she held, then looked up. "I've been too tied up with my doctoral studies to get involved with someone special. This trip is supposed to be a sort of respite from the history books I've been buried under. And of course, it's thrilling to actually see the trail again."

"Again?"

"I lived in Missouri when I was young and visited Independence with my cousins a few times. I'm not really such a stranger to these parts."

"You grew up under a sky this big?" Coni gave her a quizzical look.

"In the Ozarks, actually."

"Well, your years pursuing an Ivy League education have certainly rubbed off on you, my friend."

"What do you mean?" Johanna asked.

"This is your vacation. You could stand to loosen up a bit. Do you realize you've got your blouse buttoned almost to your neck?"

Johanna touched the collar of her tailored shirt. "I bought bright colors just for the trip," she said in a defensive tone.

"Your colors are great, but everything is so . . . so controlled. Make yourself more approachable. Unfasten a few buttons, roll up your sleeves, let your hair out of that braid when you get back to the wagon. Do you always wear those pearl earrings?"

"I never take them off," Johanna said, her hand moving farther upward. "The pearls were a gift. Heirlooms."

"I wasn't telling you to take them off," Coni said with a laugh. "They look beautiful next to your skin. But if you're going to wear them around the camp, just make sure the rest of you looks casual. You appear a little wooden at times. Just relax."

Wooden? Johanna felt suddenly self-conscious. She didn't mind a little honest criticism about her wardrobe, but Coni seemed to be implying there was a rigidity that went beyond clothes.

"Please don't be upset." Coni stopped her horse and looked Johanna in the eye. "You're a beautiful, intelligent woman. I can understand getting caught up in your studies. I watched my husband go through the same thing. Goals are important, but don't forget to have some fun."

"I danced last night."

"With Mr. Rotini. I remember. You smiled a lot." Coni winked. "Did you bring any pretty dresses with you? Sundresses? Swirling cotton skirts? Ruffles, frills? Anything like that?"

Johanna shrugged. "There's my gold dress, but it's hardly frilly. And the outfit I wore to the square dance."

Coni shook her head. "Next time we have a square dance, I'll loan you one of my dresses. You're a little taller than I am, but it'll fit. It seems a shame to let this romantic setting go to waste. I love Atlanta, but believe me, I'm going to relish every second I spend out here."

Johanna smiled at Coni but remained quiet for a moment as she absorbed her riding companion's words. Was there a veiled hint about Freddy in Coni's comment, or was Johanna simply imagining it?

"Thanks for the offer. And I'll keep what you said in mind," Johanna answered in a near-whisper just as the lunch call was sounded from the wagon train.

The teams were already unhitched and the wagons positioned in a circle that offered welcome protection from the overhead sun as members of the train lined up for box lunches and cold beverages. It was time for the "nooning," as the pioneers had called the daily break from the midday heat.

Relaxing in the shade of the wagon he now shared with Johanna, Freddy bit into his roast beef sandwich and gave silent thanks for the talent and efficiency of the cook, James LaVish.

As a member of the crew, the wagon master was privileged to be one of the first in line. Freddy had felt guilty about this protocol before, but today he saw one advantage. The circle of wagons allowed him a clear view of his fellow adventurers as they lined up to get their box lunches and beverages, then settled beside their wagons to eat.

Freddy hoped it would prove to be an opportunity to observe Johanna Remington—or rather, her mood. What in hell had gone wrong that morning? He'd thought she'd be delighted to have a new partner aboard her wagon, someone who would help with the chores and keep her company. Judging from the way she'd stalked off, his new roommate wasn't too thrilled about his methods of mediation.

"I'm taking terrible good care of your dog, Mr. Rotini." A small voice intruded on Freddy's thoughts and his visual search for Johanna.

Tiffany-with-two-little-*f*s was standing a short distance away, holding her box lunch over her head nonchalantly as Poco danced in circles around her small body.

"Gosh, Tiffany, are you sure he's not too much trouble?" Freddy watched the scene with a mixture of amusement and concern. Was his sister's dog capable of becoming more spoiled than he presently was? Would the child ever get a chance to eat? And why was this Chihuahua, who had clung to him for two days, suddenly acting as though Freddy didn't exist?

"He knows some new tricks," Tiffany announced with pride.

"Really?" Freddy slapped his thigh, producing a light cloud of dust. "You must be a good trainer," he commented with a cough. "I couldn't teach him a thing. What kind of tricks?"

"He begs real good. And each time he does it, I give him some of my food."

"Begging?" Freddy repeated. He was paying this child to baby-sit his sister's dog, and the kid was reinforcing Poco's worst habit.

"Oh-oh. I have to go. My mom's calling me." Tiffany started to skip off, her burnished curls bouncing with each step. "When I bring Poco back tonight, he'll be the bestest beggar in the whole country!"

"Great," Freddy moaned when the child was out of earshot. Tiffany's visit had distracted him. He searched the stragglers lining up for lunch. Johanna wasn't among them. Had he missed his chance to apologize before they had to spend the night together?

He looked down at his half-eaten sandwich. "If Johanna continues to snub me," Freddy muttered, "I might need some pointers from the 'bestest beggar' on how to get Miss Manifest Destiny on speaking terms again."

"Damn!"

It was the first word Freddy had heard from Johanna since morning. He hadn't even seen her approach the wagon when they'd arrived at tonight's campsite. Dropping the block of wood he was using to secure the wagon wheel, he boosted himself up on the driver's seat and peered inside.

Johanna was standing behind the wagon, her face hovering over a pan of water that rested just inside. It was obvious she had paused while washing the trail dust from her face with a washcloth. Her long dark hair was arranged in a lose braid that hung down over her shoulder. The shoulder was almost visible to Freddy because Johanna had unfastened the top buttons of her blouse.

"Damn, how could I have forgotten?" she muttered.

"You sound upset. Anything I can do to help, partner?" Freddy offered from his vantage point at the other end of the wagon.

Johanna clutched the front of her blouse before realizing she was still modestly covered.

"What's wrong?" Freddy asked.

"Isn't it obvious, Mr. Wagon Master?My yeast went wild!"

Freddy raised an eyebrow. "I—I—" His confusion ended when he spotted the bowl of bread dough Johanna had been kneading that morning. It had doubled and tripled and perhaps quadrupled in size, resting in a sticky blob over a portion of his personal possessions. He jumped down from the driver's platform and stood at Johanna's side in a matter of seconds.

"I don't believe it. I think it's still growing." Movie titles came to mind. *The Blob That Ate Wagon Number Ten*.

"I feel terrible. I'm really sorry, Freddy—" Johanna turned to apologize. "I played equestrienne all day and forgot about my most important chore." After dropping the washcloth in the pan of water and setting the basin on the ground, she climbed inside the narrow expanse of the wagon to survey the damage.

"It didn't get on your bedroll," she said, attempting to reassure him. "But I'm afraid this little stereo playback gadget and the tapes are ruined, and—"

"Oh, no!" Freddy climbed in beside her. "Poco's lullaby."

"What?"

"Nothing. It—it's not valuable. Don't worry."

"I feel terrible. I'll get this cleaned up. Maybe I put in too much yeast. I have trouble keeping my mind on domestic chores—"

"I think your kneading-while-angry technique might have done the trick." Freddy turned toward her.

They were kneeling side by side in the cramped space. Another button on her blouse had come undone, and his eyes were drawn to the swell of Johanna's breast and the tempting shadows that shifted with her movements. He cleared his throat. "You were more than just a little angry with me this morning, weren't you?"

"Yes, I was." Johanna punched down the dough in the bowl and dropped handfuls of the gooey excess on top. "You were arrogant and presumptuous. I'm perfectly capable of handling this wagon alone. B—but I—" She was suddenly hesitant. "Let's leave it at that, all right? The ride was cathartic."

"So you'll let me stay in your wagon?"

"After this accident with . . . my dough, it might be a question of whether you'll stay with me, Freddy."

Johanna glanced over at her roommate. The interior of the wagon was bathed in the warm ethereal glow of sunset. The shadow of his beard made his handsome features appear more rugged. The sun and wind had turned his face a darker shade of bronze, but her attention was drawn to his eyes. Beneath the tendril curling on his forehead, Freddy's dark eyes were filled with a strange new light.

"You'll sleep on the ground outside, of course," she added quickly.

"Remington! Wagon number ten!" a loud male voice interrupted, causing them both to turn around in the narrow interior. James LaVish, dressed in a starched apron and chef's hat, stood outside the wagon, hands on his ample hips. "You were supposed to supply me with two loaves of bread dough for tonight's dinner an hour ago, Remington!"

"She . . . well, we can't," Freddy said matter-of-factly.

"I'm speaking to the guilty party, Mr. Rotini. You may be the wagon master, but I'm responsible for the cuisine around here, and no one interferes with my menu plans." The cook addressed Johanna. "I'm waiting for my dough. Supper will be late as it is."

"I'm sorry, Mr. LaVish." Johanna felt she had done nothing but apologize for the last ten minutes. "I forgot."

"You forgot?'"

"I forgot to punch it down and form the skillet loaves." She lifted a doughy hand upward, then nodded toward the pasty glue that clung to Freddy's belongings.

She cringed at the expression on the temperamental chef's features. She half expected to be ordered to bed without supper. Freddy climbed out of the wagon and stood in silence, brushing his boot in the dust.

"This sort of thing never would have happened when my father was wagon master," James hissed beneath his breath.

"It's human to make mistakes," Freddy interjected. "And Johanna is human." He looked up at her. She was leaning out the back of the wagon, framed by the white circle of canvas. Her loose braid had unraveled into a mass of shimmering ebony waves. Her eyes were bright with emotion, and the swell of her unfettered breasts was all too visible to his appreciative gaze. At the moment, Freddy himself felt more human than he cared to admit.

James LaVish threw his hands up and stormed off, muttering something about greenhorns and kitchen duty while Freddy extended his arms upward to help Johanna to the ground.

"I believe you were washing the trail dust off when I interrupted you," he said softly. "I'll get back to securing the wagon and leave you in privacy."

Johanna saw the small patches of bread dough her hands had left on his shoulders and laughed as she tried to pull them off. "I'm not going to eat bread for the rest of the trip!" she vowed with mock anger. "In this heat, what dough is left will keep doubling in size and overtake us in our sleep and we'll smother in each other's arms."

She realized her mistake too late. "That's just a figure of speech people sometimes use—in Missouri," she added hastily, then turned away, picked up her basin of water from the ground, and resumed her cleanup.

Carrying his supper tray, Freddy waited near the beverage table until members of the train had moved through the food line. Wandering around the bustling camp, he searched for dinner companions. With a polite nod, he sat down next to a pragmatist, and they were soon joined by the train's resident realist and immaterial idealist. Within half an hour, Freddy couldn't get a word in if he tried.

"Art should be a part of every person's life, rather than being held captive in museums for viewing by a selective few."

"I thought we were still working on a definition of beauty—"

"This is only a ten-day trip. We don't have time to apply deductive reasoning to everything."

"Save it for the classroom. As I was saying, if a person is used to living in a city, surrounded by culture, then suddenly they're thrust into the environs of the Midwest and a wagon train, is their definition of beauty altered?"

As the philosophers' vociferous discussion about the nature of beauty continued through dessert and coffee, Freddy wondered if his experiment in social engineering was creating more questions than answers.

It didn't matter. He understood. These debates were not arguments. The pragmatist, idealist, and realist were sharing their ideas and gaining new perspectives. At some point in the last twenty-four hours, the two women and the lone male had each told Freddy they had finally found the perfect vacation.

They had also told him that afternoon that Professer Harold Billings was welcome in the philosopher's camp. Harold sat a short distance away, next to the idealist, sipping tea while he listened with rapt attention to the exchange of views, adding a point of his own from time to time.

Freddy felt it was his duty to make sure each of his passengers, even Harold Billings, was comfortable. The wagon master stood and took a few steps toward the professor.

"So, Harold, are you contented with your new sleeping arrangements?" Freddy asked in a low voice that wouldn't disturb the conversation of the others.

Professor Billings set his cup down on the bench and stood up. "The arrangements will be quite adequate," Harold said stiffly. "I have always found philosophy majors to be exceedingly kind."

"I'll take that as a compliment."

"You hold a degree?"

"A master's from UC at Berkeley."

Professor Billings rocked back on his heels. "I don't know what to say."

"Look, Harold"— Freddy touched the other man's shoulder lightly—"about this morning. I'm not going to interfere in personal business between you and Johanna, but I hope you work your differences out soon."

"I—I'll wait until she's gotten over the pain of rejection before I talk with her." Harold's voice was suddenly subdued.

"Rejection?"

"Yes. I'm sure she's rapidly becoming aware of how difficult the journey will be without a well-informed roommate, a person with a solid knowledge of the Oregon Trail."

The man was impossible. Freddy didn't want to display his temper in front of the others. He smiled politely. "Johanna hasn't sensed the intellectual void of your leaving yet. Perhaps it's because I'm not her only roommate."

"Wh—what? Is she inviting the rest of the crew—"

"No." Freddy shrugged. "You'd forgotten about Poco."

Because supper ran late, the tall tales had to be cut short. After the last story Freddy made a few announcements to the group, picked up Poco and the dog's assorted toys from Tiffany's campsite, and returned to the wagon. He was anxious to see Johanna. He'd spotted her sitting with the Cameron and Wong families during dinner, and later she'd joined the elderly couple from California around the campfire.

He heard her moving about inside the wagon, humming softly. Setting the Chihuahua and the dog's rubber hamburger on the ground, he knocked on the side of the wagon before peeking inside.

"Have a nice evening, Johanna?"

"It was wonderful," she said with enthusiasm. She was kneeling on the planked floor. "I'm meeting some nice people and making friends. And supper was good, even if there wasn't enough bread for everyone. And we all know whose fault that was." Her tone was playful and self-mocking. She turned to the chore of turning one of the wagon benches into a narrow bed—two feet of hard wood. "You were your normal gregarious self, Freddy. I swear you can talk to anyone. The people on the train really like you."

Talk to anyone? He raised an eyebrow. Perhaps he'd been overly concerned about seeking approval from the crew. Freddy hadn't given much thought to whether the rest of the people on the train saw their wagon master in a favorable light. He was just being himself... a man with a degree in philosophy who'd spent ten years driving a truck.

Plato on eighteen wheels, the other truckers had

called him, shortening the good-natured teasing to Plato for his CB handle. Ten years ago, fresh out of college, he'd traveled the interstates and back roads in search of the real America. He'd hauled freight from city to city, state to state, sleeping in the small berth in the back of his cab while each of his old friends and classmates in turn seemed to settle down in one city, one job, one home. Slowly they'd married or entered long relationships, making him feel the odd man out.

The road had brought its rewards. He'd developed a network of friends across the country, an extended family of truckers, farmers, business associates, restaurateurs, students of philosophy, and like-minded people.

And of course, there had been women. But, necessarily, the relationships had been short-lived. Freddy discovered he shared the protective streak he'd witnessed in his five older brothers, and he lost valuable time on the road by having to stop and call whatever woman was on his mind to assure himself she was safe while he traveled.

Was he being fair to Johanna? Freddy pondered. Was he really being himself? What about the boots, the swagger, and the drawl? No, he was trying to romanticize his newly acquired role. He watched her struggle with the bunk inside the wagon.

"Did it occur to you," Freddy ventured, "that the ground might be more comfortable than that narrow instrument of torture. It's a warm night. Why not bring your bedroll outside and sleep under the stars?"

"If I do, I won't be able to catch up on my reading."

"You can read in the wagon tomorrow—and leave the driving to the crew."

"And miss all the sights?"

"Come on. The night air will do you good," Freddy urged. "And we can talk."

"It's not very private out there."

"There aren't any walls, but it *is* on the dark side of the wagon."

"Well, I guess I could catch up on my reading another time . . ." There was reticence in her tone. She seemed to be studying the bunk. "The ground might be a comfortable alternative."

The bedrolls were soon laid out, separated by half a foot of sparse grassland. Extra blankets were piled nearby. Freddy hesitated as he looked at the clothes he'd packed. The crew wore little to bed and he'd become accustomed to the practice. What would be tasteful attire in mixed company? He decided on a pair of comfortable drawstring pants and a sweatshirt.

Johanna tightened the back opening of the canvas and sat on the floor of the wagon to change from her jeans to the loose velour jogging pants and jacket she used as sleepwear.

She stepped outside. Freddy had already tucked himself into his sleeping bag, his back to the wagon. He was singing softly to the small Chihuahua who lay on a blanket next to him.

Not wanting to embarrass her traveling companion, Johanna quietly slipped between the thick layers of her bedroll, which had mysteriously moved closer to her roommate's sleeping bag in her absence. She listened to the lilting lullaby with interest. There was nothing foolish about this scene between man and dog. The wagon master had obviously been saddled with a very spoiled dog who would make the trip seem very long.

"Sorry, I didn't know you'd be ready so soon," Freddy whispered when Poco had settled. He explained the lullaby ritual the dog insisted on.

"You must be a very understanding brother to take on a burden like Poco." Johanna couldn't suppress a smile. "I'm sorry if my mistake forced you to give live performances from now on. Maybe with all this excitement, Poco will forget the evening routine and act like a—a normal dog."

"I doubt that," Freddy said with a sigh. He looked upward. "It's clear tonight. Have you studied the stars? Looks like a good night for making wishes."

"Hmmmmm, beautiful, aren't they?" she answered sleepily. "They seem closer out here. I can't see much of the sky back east." But then how often had she taken the time to step out of her ivory tower in search of stars . . . or wishes?

"Go ahead, make a wish," Freddy urged.

He watched as Johanna closed her eyes. He'd listened to four opinionated people discuss the nature of beauty over dinner that evening. They had wasted their time. Beauty was subjective and often fleeting.

Johanna was beautiful. There hadn't been a moment when he'd thought otherwise. But tonight was different.

Nothing the philosophers had said held the power of this one moment. The moment of watching Johanna make a wish. The deep olive tone of her skin was set off by the soft pink velour of her collar. Her ebony hair fell in lustrous waves on her pillow, inviting his touch.

He found himself making his own silent wishes. A string of them.

Johanna opened her eyes and glanced at Freddy. He was watching her intently. "Can you imagine," she asked in a whisper, "being a real pioneer? Camping out beside your wagon, not knowing what waited for you beyond the darkness or the next dawn? Not really knowing what vast undeveloped territory you were going to call home or whether you'd arrive with family intact . . . or alone . . . or not at all. They must have made wishes *here*, Freddy, under these stars. The people traveled on, planted little star seeds and made those wishes come true."

Her eyes filled with tears at the thought of the pioneer women, forced to swallow their fear and follow their men. "I think the thing that drew me to the Oregon Trail for my doctorate was courage," she whispered.

"Do you like taking risks, Johanna? Would you have joined the hordes that reacted to the hype and headed west in 1843?"

An actual date. She was impressed. The wagon master had progressed in his knowledge of the trail. "Some of them were escaping economic disaster in the East—"

Freddy put a finger to her lips. "That was hardly what I wanted to hear. I asked whether you were willing to take risks. Is that tomboy from Missouri still struggling to get out? Was little Joey Remington courageous?"

Johanna wrapped her fingers around his hand and lifted it gently away from her mouth. A moment in her childhood stood still. A private moment that no person should ever have had to face. The images were frozen tableaux that would not move forward or backward in her mind. Still frame. Her fingers entwined through his.

"A brave child doesn't always grow into a brave adult." It was a long time before she could form the words. "I—I want this journey to be a chance to test myself, Freddy. I didn't want you to move into my wagon because I was afraid you'd turn into an overprotective male."

"I promise. If a herd of wild boars rampaged through the camp right now, I wouldn't attempt to do a thing." His remark drew a smile.

His fingertips touched and lingered along the edge of her jawline before his thumb moved in a tantalizing pattern over the fullness of her lower lip. Her mouth parted.

"Besides a protector, was there anything else you didn't want me to turn into?" he asked before his mouth brushed hers in a soft intimate caress of lips. Freddy heard her sharp intake of breath.

"A diversion, a distraction." Her voice was strangled but he heard the words clearly—just before Johanna's hand reached up and tangled in his hair. She was pulling his mouth downward.

And she was thinking. What had Coni said about her being too "wooden"? How ironic. At this moment, it was all too true. Johanna felt like a balsa wood puppet—what invisible power controlled her hands, her mouth, her heart?

"You don't want distractions? My God, Johanna. Don't you"—Freddy tried to speak—"find this rather . . . distracting?"

There was no answer. The third kiss began without the gentle dalliance of the first two. Freddy moaned softly as he probed the soft, sweet recesses of Johanna's mouth and felt her hands move under his sweatshirt and over his naked back.

Their fourth and final kiss was a slow gentle breaking away. They held each other in silence before Freddy moved his sleeping bag, closing the short distance between them. Their pillows were touching but not overlapping. Their fingers remained entwined.

Neither spoke for minutes. He could see the luminous shimmer of her eyes in the faint glow of the train's communal firelight. The warm flickering reflection from the campfire shone beneath their wagon to the outer darkness where they lay, illuminating the need in Johanna's gaze.

"*That* was star seed, Joey." He moved her hand upward and kissed her palm.

"Star seed, Freddy? That implies there's going to be a harvest." Her voice was a soft silken whisper. As he watched, her lips curved in a smile before she closed her eyes and drifted into sleep.

CHAPTER FOUR

WITH SLIGHT TREPIDATION, Freddy began to teach Johanna how to harness their team of horses after breakfast the following morning. He found her close feminine presence more disturbing in the pink hues of dawn.

After washing up in the privacy of the wagon, she emerged looking radiant, without makeup, wisps of damp dark hair curling around her face. The sleeves of her raw silk shirt were gathered in loose folds around her elbows. The top three buttons were undone, exposing the soft shadows of her neck and upper chest. Though she was tall, her bone structure was slight, her wrists small, her hands strong but delicate.

Each time he moved close to explain the harnessing procedure, he caught the fragrance of the soap she had bathed with. The elusive scent made him think of childhood walks in the woods in his native

Oregon. Sweet wildflowers and rising sap. No one in the crew wagon smelled like that.

Stop it, he told himself as forbidden images came to mind of Johanna bathing alone in the wagon.

He focused on the horses and continued the lesson with new resolve, but shivers of awareness continued to course through him whenever his movements caused his callused fingertips to brush the soft skin of Johanna's hands. She was quick to shift away, but when her eyes met his, there was a hint of mischief in their gray depths.

"The horses are a little skittish today, aren't they?" Johanna remarked as Freddy tightened one of the straps and a ripple of protest ran through the team.

"I could probably say the same thing about you." Freddy paused in his work to study her upturned face. The two of them had exchanged few words since they'd awoken.

The intimacy they had shared the night before had shifted into this vague uneasiness.

Freddy blamed himself. It wasn't just the scented soap, the sensuous shadows, or the sunrise in Johanna's eyes. He'd taken her words to heart. He was leery of being too protective, too forceful in his instructions. He had just mastered the harnessing technique himself.

At moments like this, he felt like confessing everything: *Johanna, let me be honest. It's all a joke. I might look confident, but I'm a novice, a neophyte, a phony, a fraud . . .*

She learned quickly and seemed determined to demonstrate her skill and strength at every task.

"Me skittish?" Johanna looked surprised. "I'm just

concentrating... on the lesson. I'd like to be able to do this alone tomorrow."

He was startled by her assumption. Even the more experienced teamsters frequently handled the harnessing in pairs.

"Don't you think you're expecting too much of yourself? You're just beginning to understand the technique, and it'd take too long to do it alone."

"How long did it take you to learn?" Johanna interjected.

"Th—that's beside the point. The fact is, I'm your partner on this trip. We'll do it together or let the assigned driver and one of the mule skinners do it." He changed the subject back to the tedious process of harnessing a team of horses.

"I'd also like a chance to drive the wagon myself."

Freddy tightened his grip on the leather reins and stared with amazement at the woman who stood a short distance away. The defiance in Johanna's voice was reflected in her stance. To hell with the shadows of her throat. He was going to have to deal with the total woman.

She had told him last night that this trip would be her proving ground. Freddy wondered if it might be his undoing. On one hand, he had twelve ounces of spoiled, dependent dog in his care, and on the other, he had an independent woman determined to test her survival skills. And every time she challenged herself with learning a new skill, she would be putting him to a test as well. He'd have to become more observant if he was going to keep up with her.

"Harnessing the team, driving the wagon—is there anything else you want to rush into, Johanna?"

Freddy stepped away from the horses, his hands resting gently on his hips.

"Everything else can wait." There was a soft echo of challenge in her voice.

"Everything?" One of Freddy's hands moved downward to the top of his leg. His fingers drummed against the taut denim on his upper thigh. "What about us?"

"Boss, it's time to move out. Charlie and the guys need your help up front figuring out the placement of the wagons for this morning's journey," a male voice interrupted. The wagon master turned to face the intruder. The young driver assigned to their wagon was frowning as he inspected the half-completed harnessing job.

"Josh, I was showing Ms. Remington how to prepare the team. I won't have time"— Freddy cast a questioning glance at Johanna—"to finish . . . until tonight."

Johanna watched as Freddy picked up the remainder of the thick leather and handed it to the driver. The two men spoke briefly about the nooning site and the grade of road they'd cover before the midday meal.

She wished there was time to tell Freddy everything that was on her mind, to confront him with the truth: how she knew he hadn't earned the title of wagon master and it was all a ruse. But her purpose wasn't to disgrace him in any way. She simply wanted to convince Freddy to admit his novice status and ignorance to the passengers on the train. Maybe he wasn't an expert on the history of the Oregon Trail, but he was a master at making her fellow passengers feel at ease. They'd accept him as a wagon master in training and give Charlie, the lead driver, the respect he deserved.

That part of it could be easy. But there was more. Freddy was a master at awakening longings she thought she had buried long ago. His physical resemblance to Ronnie Buck Ferguson was uncanny. Both men had wavy black hair, expressive brown eyes, dark complexions, and easy smiles.

Freddy was an older, more mature version of the only man she had ever loved. But it was Freddy's humor and sensitivity, not his appearance, that made her recall the pleasure and the pain she had shared with Ronnie Buck.

Was she being fair to Freddy Rotini? How could she distinguish memories of an old love, a childhood friend turned sweetheart, from the wild, chaotic emotions she was experiencing now? She was almost thirty. Why wasn't she able to put those painful lessons learned so long ago to use? It was time to create new memories, but the fear of being hurt made her more hesitant than she wanted to be.

Freddy tipped his hat and gave her an uncertain smile before he headed toward his position at the front of the wagon train. Johanna found herself raising her hand upward to mimic his gesture before she could stop herself.

"How are your space cowboys today?" Johanna ran through the tall grass to catch up with Coni Cameron, who was walking alongside the wagon train, singing softly.

Coni greeted her with a smile. In two days, they had managed to develop a surprisingly close friendship. The proximity of their wagons and the lazy hours of walking and riding provided ample time for talking.

"I'll tell you about the status of my little cowboys, but you've got to promise to keep it a secret. They don't want the other kids to know."

"I promise." Johanna said with a laugh. "What's up?"

"Captain Orion and Mercron the Meteoroid would die of shame if anyone found out they've run out of energy stabilizers and have been forced to adjust their techno-metabolizers for two hours."

"I take it that means you've got two tired cowboys taking an afternoon nap in the wagon?"

"Very good. Evidently we're going to make camp early today so people can do some fishing, riding, and hiking. There's supposed to be some firearm demonstration . . . pioneer style, of course. My kids are excited but willing to take a nap, because they don't want to miss the wagon master's history lesson."

"Freddy's teaching h—history?"

"I'm surprised he didn't tell you. He gathered the kids together yesterday outside the crew wagon and held an impromptu class. He told them what life was like for youngsters when the Oregon Trail was young."

"Freddy?"

"Did you know that some of the families carried chickens in crates under their wagons?" Coni began gesturing with her hands as she related Freddy's lesson. "The chickens would graze with the cattle, then run back to their crates at hitching time because it was the only home they knew. I bet those fresh eggs were appreciated."

"Chickens?" Johanna repeated.

"And my youngest thinks he'll be a wagon scout when he grows up," Coni continued on enthusiastically, "because he says the scout must be the one who runs out for hamburgers and fries. He figures there are so many people on a wagon train that no one will notice if he sneaks a few fries out of the bag."

Johanna couldn't resist a smile. "Did Freddy tell the kids the pioneers *ran out* for hamburgers?"

"Oh, no. He told them about all the things kids did to help their families, like gathering firewood, picking up buffalo chips for building fires, carrying water, entertaining themselves inside the wagon when it rained, and stuffing wet boots with grass."

Johanna was speechless for a moment. "W—what topic is our wagon master speaking on today?"

"I'm not sure—" Coni reached inside the back pocket of her jeans. She pulled out a sheet of paper. "Let me check."

"What's that?" Using her height advantage, Johanna peered over her companion's shoulder, scanning the hand-scrawled list of topics.

"It's a series of talks our Mr. Rotini's going to give the kids. Today he'll focus on—"

"Courage: why the pioneers of yesterday are like today's astronauts," Johanna finished. She whistled beneath her breath. "Is this mandatory?"

"No," Coni said with a shrug. "But the kids love to listen to Freddy talk. While he's speaking, he uses clay to demonstrate a point."

"What did he do yesterday—form little chickens and buffalo chips?" Johanna tried to imagine Freddy working figures of clay while surrounded by a rapt audience of children, but unbidden images of white fringe and a dark curl came to mind.

"By the way, I approve."

"Of what?"

"You let your hair down and rolled up your sleeves. It's a change for the better. And that touch of blush looks good on you."

"What blush?" Johanna touched her cheek.

"You mean it's natural?" Coni put her hands on her hips and pretended to study Johanna. "Looks like something's got you in a fever . . . which prompts me to ask: How are things working out with your new roommate?"

Johanna told Coni about the runaway bread dough, Poco's lullaby ritual, and sleeping under the stars. She omitted any mention of the stirring kisses she'd shared with Freddy, or the wagon master's lack of credentials. During the silence that followed, she worried that her words had carried implications that could be misconstrued. She recalled the way fellow passengers were reacting to the pairing up of couples from the singles' wagons.

Her walking companion had strayed ahead of her. Johanna struggled to find the words that might express her feelings about the situation as she doubled her steps to catch up with Coni.

"I'm not sure how this looks to other people"—Johanna touched the sleeve of Coni's pullover top—"but I didn't come on this journey in search of a man. I doubt if I could ever be more than . . . a close friend with Freddy."

"Is that so?" Coni folded up the schedule of talks for kids and stuck it in her back pocket. "What makes you say that?"

"Goals."

"Goals?"

"Yes, I have short- and long-term goals. Once I reach them, I'll have time for other pursuits." Johanna didn't care to detail her other concerns—like the effect Freddy's vulnerability had on her or the secret she knew about his acquisition of the wagon train.

"Maybe I was wrong, Johanna," Coni said in a teasing tone. "Maybe you should button your blouse to the top button and pull your hair into a bun after all."

"B—but—"

"What about personal goals?" Coni asked with a smile. "Call them dreams if you like. Lord knows they don't always happen in the order you plan. Things just happen . . . if you let them."

"And you think I should 'let them'?"

Coni turned to face Johanna. "I don't know if you're trying to convince *me* or *yourself* that you have no feelings for Freddy."

"I don't even know him that well, but from what I've seen, it's not hard to figure out we're very different. Opposites!" Johanna threw up her hands. "Freddy is well educated and intelligent, but there's another side to him. He's funny and easygoing. I'm more . . . serious and goal-oriented."

"There's that word again," Coni said as she widened her eyes. "You haven't had time to find out what the man wants in his future. Good Lord, his dreams could be loftier than yours."

The two women continued walking in silence. In the distance they could hear the faint laughter of children, the low rumble of wagon wheels on the hard dusty ground, and the occasional whinny of a horse. Coni sighed, looked down at the ground, and shook her head before speaking again.

"Why don't you just follow your instincts? Let all those feelings bubble to the surface. In the city, we have a lot of rules. I guess we need them if we're going to have some semblance of order. But this"—she pointed upward to the clear blue ceiling of sky—"is different. Where you and I live, we're not going to get too many chances to see so far ahead of where we're going. Come on, Johanna. Doesn't this huge sky make you feel like spreading your arms and doing something crazy?"

Johanna stopped walking. "Something crazy?" She cocked an eyebrow. "Like getting involved with Freddy Rotini?"

"Why, that's the sanest thing I've heard you say since I met you." Coni laughed and, spreading her arms wide, embraced Johanna.

"Courage is overcoming your fear of doing something that scares you. Some of the pioneers on the Oregon Trail didn't know where they were going to live and how they would survive once they got there. Some turned back—they went home—"

It was the most unusual classroom Johanna had ever seen. Freddy Rotini sat propped against an elm tree, surrounded by a ring of mesmerized children. As he talked about conquering the fear of the unknown, he formed a very realistic spaceship out of clay. Poco sat in Freddy's lap, vying for attention.

As Johanna eavesdropped from behind a fallen log, the lesson progressed to include mention of present-day astronauts. Freddy was making analogies that had never occurred to her. She was impressed. Rising gracefully from her position in the grass, she walked back toward the wagon pondering the situation.

Was it necessary to ask Freddy to confess his masquerade? Did it really matter? Was he doing any harm? She was so involved in her thoughts that she almost ran into Charlie Vishtek, lead driver for the train.

"Excuse me," Johanna apologized.

"No offense taken, ma'am," the grizzled old man said with a slight nod of the head. "You're an expert on the trail, Ms. Remington. How's our wagon master doin' with the lesson over t'ere?"

"In my opinion, his technique is a little unorthodox, but the kids love him." Johanna told Charlie about the subject of today's lecture. As she spoke, a thought flashed through her mind. The short weathered man at her side had once held the title of wagon master. If he resented Freddy, it didn't show.

Charlie ran a hand through his white hair. He smiled and chuckled softly while Johanna related today's lesson. "Well, as long as he gits the facts right, he's doin' no harm. I thought he was a fool, buying all that clay back near Sutherland. But I guess the man has a purpose after all."

"Yes, I'm sure he does," Johanna said softly before she turned and headed to camp, where she was assigned to kitchen duty for the second time.

The harmonica player was blowing a lively tune and two of the mule skinners were performing a frolicking jig for the post-supper crowd when the sky opened up without warning. The campfire sputtered as the torrential downpour, whipped by the wind, turned the dry dusty camp into a pool of mud.

Coffee and hot chocolate spilled from tin cups as panicked wagoneers jumped up from the benches, surprised by the sudden storm. Lightning creased the night sky, illuminating the chaotic scene within the camp's circle.

"Grab some extra blocks. Make sure all the wagons are leveled!" Charlie's voice competed with the low rumble of thunder. The crew scattered in all directions as passengers gathered their senses and ran for cover.

Freddy picked up the Wongs' bawling two-year-old and held his jacket over the baby girl's head, crushing her to his chest as he followed the child's frantic parents and three older siblings through the rain. After situating the Wongs, Freddy ran from wagon to wagon to make sure each passenger was accounted for and to check for leaks in the canvas or a need for supplies.

The wind slapped against wood and cloth, threatening to send the fleet of prairie schooners through the uncharted sea of mud that was accumulating throughout the camp. A sentry was chosen from the crew to watch for any rise in the nearby Platte River.

"Is everyone accounted for?" Freddy bellowed into the philosophers' wagon. He was surprised to find Professor Harold Billings sitting on one of the fold-down benches inside, his hand resting on the thigh of the pragmatist. The woman was drying Harold's hair with a towel. The idealist and realist appeared to have similar ideas. An aura of intimacy was evident between both couples.

"Everyone comfortable in here?" Freddy inquired.

A discussion about the nature of comfort started immediately. Freddy shrugged and tightened the canvas opening as a protective measure—for those within and those outside—before moving on to the next wagon. And the next.

Frightened livestock vied with panicked passengers for attention as a series of thunderbolts rocked the camp, followed by another siege of torrential rain, allowing the crew no respite from their muddy labor.

Freddy had never found the need to test his leadership. He had relied heavily on Charlie's expertise. But the crisis called for calm thinking and quick decisions. While Charlie shouted instructions two hundred yards away, Freddy found himself alone in his duties, surrounded by anxious faces. Though his own heart was beating double time, it seemed these people found something in his expression or in his voice that calmed them.

Two hours later, the rain had slackened slightly. The crew assured the passengers that the wagons were leveled and the livestock safe. Wet, sore, and tired, Freddy stumbled through the mud to his own wagon.

"Johanna! It's Freddy!" He gave a warning cry before peering inside the back opening in the canvas.

He hardly recognized the woman that stared back at him.

Johanna's wet hair was hanging in tiny curling strands around her face and shoulder. Her light pink blouse molded to her curves like a second skin. Her nipples stood out dark against the wet fabric.

Freddy swallowed hard as he removed his mud-caked boots. His protective urges mingled with less virtuous desires as he climbed inside. "You're cold," he announced softly. "Why didn't you find a blanket? I thought you'd be dried off by now and rolled up in a sleeping bag."

"I just got here myself," Johanna explained as she searched the overhead canvas for leaks. "I was helping some of the families get their kids to the bathroom and back, changed into dry clothes, and settled. The little ones were terribly upset."

"I think we could both use a blanket," Freddy said as he reached out and touched her arm. Johanna's thin blouse offered even less protection than his flannel shirt. If he was numb with cold, she had to be chilled to the bone.

"I'm afraid I might have given all the blankets away." A shiver was evident in her voice. "But I could have missed one. Let me rummage through the supplies again."

Freddy was surprised by this side of Johanna. He'd seen her running through the camp a few times during the storm but there hadn't been time to ask questions. He'd assumed she was searching for items for herself or their wagon.

"Do we have any towels?" he asked as water dripped from his forehead onto the planked floor.

"Two." Johanna handed him one towel.

Freddy accepted the rectangle of terry cloth and wondered how it could possibly absorb all the water he'd collected in the past two hours.

"Well, at least our bedrolls are dry," he muttered with a sigh. When Johanna didn't respond, he glanced up. "Our bedrolls *are* dry, aren't they?"

"When I lifted the blankets out of the wagon, I accidentally got my hand tangled in the cords of your bedroll and it tumbled out the back and opened up on the ground. By the time I put the blankets back, it was too late."

"It's wet?"

"Soaked. It's turned into a sort of soggy, muddy waterbed. I'm really sorry about that, Freddy."

"Maybe I should rephrase my questions. What *do* we have, Johanna?"

"My sleeping bag and the two towels."

"Why aren't you drying yourself off with the other towel?" Freddy asked with concern. She was shivering visibly. The dark curly strands were turning into clusters of shiny ringlets. Her cheeks were flushed and her lips showed a tinge of blue.

"The other towel is Poco's bed." Johanna nodded toward the corner where the Chihuahua was dozing on his back. Only the dog's black nose could be seen above the swaddling of thick blue bath towel.

"Good Lord, the mutt went to sleep without the lullaby routine." Freddy smiled with relief. Johanna sneezed. "Bless you," he said in a whisper, reaching over to dry her hair and face with the least damp section of his towel, "for helping the other passengers and for sparing me an evening performance of 'Poco's Lullaby.'"

"I thought he was dead at first. He had his little feet up in the air and his tongue was hanging out . . . and for once, he wasn't panting."

Freddy thought there was irony in her remark. He wondered if his own tongue was hanging out at the moment. How could he be so affected by a drenched female whose hair was kinking up into tangled disarray? He couldn't keep his attention off her kneeling figure. When a gust of wind intruded through the opening in the canvas, the reaction of Johanna's body was clearly visible. Her breasts were outlined in detail beneath the damp fabric of her blouse.

Freddy averted his gaze. "It's getting late. We won't have to worry about Poco but I might need a lullaby since I'll be sleeping on this planked floor tonight—"

"Are you out of your mind? All the blankets have been given away and your bedroll's drying out under the wagon. We don't have a choice. You'll have t—to share my sleeping bag."

"Share a bedroll?" Freddy half choked the words. At the moment, Johanna's full lips and fascinating curves would tempt a saint.

"You don't have to sound so repulsed by the idea." Her eyes met his boldly. "I don't snore, kick, or talk in my sleep."

"Repulsed? I'm delighted by your plan."

"But there are alternatives," she offered almost too quickly. "We could sleep in shifts. Two hours on, two hours off . . . if you prefer." Her tone was reticent. "Or I could sit up and . . . write postcards, Freddy."

"If you're feeling guilty about giving all our blankets away—don't be. Desperate times call for desperate measures—"

"My bag's generously cut. In fact, I borrowed it from a faculty couple—the Doumits." She pulled the bedroll from its storage place and looked down at the tattered tag that clung to the fabric. "The Doumits claimed this bag could sleep two—*in an emergency,*" Johanna added quickly.

"Is that why you're studying that tag? To find out if our situation qualifies as an emergency? What does it say?"

"Unlawful to remove under penalty of law," she murmured, then looked up and gave him a shy smile. "I don't know why people leave these tags on—"

"What you're really asking is, how are we going to share less than three feet of bed all night? Am I right, Johanna?"

"Well, I guess this really qualifies as an emergency then, doesn't it?" She dropped the bedroll to the floor and began looking through her clothes. "Now if you'll turn your back, Mr. Rotini, I'll turn mine, and we can both change into some dry clothes and try to get some sleep."

CHAPTER FIVE

THE MOMENT OF TRUTH.

Johanna knelt next to the sleeping bag, where Freddy was positioning his body to allow room for her. He was dressed in the usual drawstring pants and sweatshirt, and she was wearing her velour jogging suit with the zippered top. But it would take armored pajamas to offer her any protection from the growing attraction she felt toward this man.

Johanna doubted if any pioneer had been faced with this particular dilemma but she had only herself to blame. It had been her idea to share the bedroll. But what else could she have done? Let him sleep on the floorboards? She was the one who had dropped his sleeping bag in the mud.

The soft lantern light accentuated Freddy's firm jaw and high cheekbones. She longed to run her finger along his nose, to ask about the bump that kept his features from being labeled perfect.

Exhaustion drew her downward to the thin cushion of comfort the bedroll offered against the wagon's hard floor. She tried to zip the side of the bag up but it wouldn't budge past her protruding knee. She would have to move closer to Freddy. She inched toward him in a backward motion and stopped suddenly. Her buttocks were pressed into the curve of his body.

The zipper inched upward, pressing her back up against the wall of his chest. The top of her head fit snugly under his chin. Generously cut? Sleeps two in an emergency? Had the Doumits lied to her?

"Are you comfortable?" Freddy asked in a muffled voice when she tried to move away from the intimate positioning of arms and legs.

"You sound funny—"

"My arms are over my head."

"Good heavens, Freddy. You can put them—" Where could he put them? "Move them into a more natural position."

"But that would be around your waist."

"Fine. Anything, if it means we'll be able to get some sleep."

Johanna felt his outer arm move downward. His hand brushed her hip lightly before settling on the soft velour covering her stomach. She could feel the heat of him wherever their bodies touched, and even in places where a thin layer of air separated them.

"Your hair smells like rain." Freddy's words formed a rush of warm wind against her neck. "I like it this way. It's like a cloud of curls run amok."

That was a compliment? Her hair had run amok. With a sigh, Johanna reached up and brushed a mutinous strand of ebony away from her cheek. "I generally use a conditioner to tame it, but when I get caught in the rain, it's hopeless. That's the problem with naturally curly hair."

"Hmmm, I hope we're in for more nasty weather," Freddy said with a chuckle. The rumble of laughter in his chest was as distracting as his velvet voice. Johanna shifted her body and found her hips lodged firmly against him. The evidence of his arousal couldn't be ignored. Their close proximity was affecting him as much as it was her.

"You're shivering. Are you still cold?" The meaning of his words was lost. She was immersed in sensations. Freddy's palm pressed against her waist, forcing her buttocks against his rigid flesh. His lips brushed her neck. Johanna couldn't suppress the moan that escaped her throat. She closed her eyes for a moment, hoping to blot out the romantic lantern light, the rustic interior of the wagon, and Freddy's disturbing presence. It didn't work. She turned slowly in his arms and looked upward into the eyes of her tormentor.

There was a devilish gleam in their depths that intrigued rather than frightened her. His long lashes still clung together in star patterns from the rain. Johanna found herself echoing his thoughts. Stormy weather would be nice if each time it brought out that look in Freddy and forced them to share such intimate quarters.

The shadow of his beard only heightened the aura of his masculinity. And that ridiculous curl had returned to dangle over his broad forehead. Whose hair had run amok? she longed to tease him. His thick black hair was a tangle of silky curls.

She remembered the gentle conversation and tender kisses they'd shared the night before. When his hand left her waist, following the path of the metal zipper that ran up her velour jogging top, she didn't stop him. Her breath caught as Freddy's fingertips touched the bare flesh above the zipper, then settled on the pull ring.

In the faint light of the lantern, she could see his brown eyes sparkling as if lit from within.

"Johanna?" he asked with more breath than voice. She answered with the pressure of her fingertips against his cheek.

Freddy's lips parted in a slight smile as his fingers tugged on the ring. Then his mouth was hovering over hers, warming the millimeter of air between them.

The zipper slid downward an inch just as his lips brushed hers. The kiss that began featherlight deepened. Johanna felt taut curls beneath her fingertips. She was burying her fingers in his hair, controlling the pressure of this kiss. Her mind raced ahead to the future—five minutes hence. How would this evening end if they both lost control? She heard the zipper moving downward and felt her nipples firm as one of her breasts was exposed to the cool air. Then Freddy's palm covered the crest of the curve and moved in tantalizing patterns over the sensitive tip.

"You're beautiful, Joey," he murmured beside her ear just as the monotony of rain against the canvas overhead was broken by the crash of thunder. Wind lashed against the side of the wagon, rattling the contents. The howling impact was followed by cries for help—then a loud crash—and the cries turned into terrified screams.

"What's going on?" Freddy tried to sit up but his

movement was slowed by the tangle of Johanna's long legs around his. As commotion erupted throughout the camp, Freddy struggled out of the sleeping bag and searched for a pair of dry jeans in his duffel bag before abandoning his effort.

Outside, men and women shouted instructions in order to be heard above the wind. Freddy pulled on his wet jeans. A child cried out in heart-gripping terror and Johanna felt her throat tighten.

"The kids, Freddy—do you think—" She wouldn't allow herself to finish the dreadful thought. Her attention was diverted by powerful flashlight beams that ricocheted off the canvas in frightening patterns. Johanna was tossed against a hickory support as the wagon shook and shuddered.

"Don't go out until you zip up that top!" Freddy gave her an anxious glance. "God, Johanna, I wish—"

"I know," she whispered, shoving her arm into a jacket sleeve.

"Boss!" Josh's anxious face appeared at the back of the canvas. "We're damn lucky! The blocks under number five gave way . . . looks like a wheel might be broke." The young driver spoke in a jumbled rush of words. "But no one's hurt . . . the wagon's on its side in the mud."

"Number five? Is everyone out?" Freddy pulled on the mud-caked boots Josh handed him.

"Isn't that the philosophers' wagon?" Johanna saw the concern etched in Freddy's features.

"Yeah. Damn! Probably weighted down by all those heavy thoughts."

His aside was lost on Josh but Johanna smiled appreciatively. "Put this on!" She tossed him a rain parka after he hit the ground. "I have the feeling it's going to be a long night."

"Great! A volunteer! I'm going to need some help!" James LaVish shouted over the downpour as he opened the back door to the chuck wagon.

"I thought you would." Johanna shook the water off her parka and stepped into the small work area. She smiled at the cook, only to meet the fierce resistance of a resentful stare.

"It's y—you!" James LaVish scowled. "Well, it's a good thing we're not making bread."

Gritting her teeth, Johanna moved around his ample form. "Thanks for the warm reception. I could have stayed in my wagon. What difference does it make who helps?" Johanna reached for the tin of coffee on the upper shelf and set it on the counter. She'd been on kitchen duty twice. No one had complained about her work. "The crew's going to need buckets of coffee before the night's over and—"

"You don't need to tell me how to feed a hungry crew, Ms. Remington. This accident with wagon number five wouldn't have happened if my father were still in charge!" James grabbed the tin away from her and tore off the lid. "Dad used to stay up all night when the rains hit, checking and rechecking every wagon. He knows the business. It's not something you learn on summer vacation."

"Are you implying Freddy Rotini is treating his responsibilities too lightly?" Johanna struggled to ignite the propane stove. The wind howled under the canopy each time she lit a match. "Damn," she muttered for the fourth time.

James LaVish took the matches from her and

shielded the flame with his body. There was a whooshing sound as blue flames leaped around the four rings. He blew out the match and spoke in a low voice. "How much do you know about what happened between Rotini and my father?"

"Freddy isn't aware that I know your father lost the wagon train in a poker game in Reno. I overheard him muttering the story to his dog." Johanna began filling the coffeepots with water while James spooned coffee into the brewing baskets. "Freddy might be something of a novice but he's eager to learn and anxious to prove himself. I think you're dead wrong about whether he can handle the job."

"You can hardly be objective, Ms. Remington. He's sleeping in your wagon."

Johanna gave the cook a wry smile. "Freddy's rules forbid a passenger from being alone in a wagon. Especially a female passenger. Personally, I thought that would increase Freddy's ratings in the eyes of his macho crew." She positioned the last pot of water on the stove.

"It takes years of experience to take on a specialized job like wagon master." James handed the brewing baskets of coffee to Johanna with a little too much force.

"Did they give courses on chuck wagon cookery in that culinary institute you keep talking about, Chef LaVish?" Johanna popped the baskets inside each coffeepot, clanging metal on metal.

James cleared his throat. "I believe we were talking about Freddy Rotini." Bang! He slammed a top down on one of the pots as if to punctuate his words. "At the moment"—bang!—"there's a wagon on its side in the mud"—bang!—"and that doesn't make our good leader look very capable"—bang!—"does it?"

Johanna was surprised by the cook's outburst. "May I ask why you have so little trust in Freddy's leadership, Mr. LaVish?"

"Because"—the chef paused, his fingers toying with the lid of one of the coffeepots—"I believe he cheated."

"Freddy, cheat?" Johanna was astonished at the thought.

"My father's an ace poker player. Never loses. He won't discuss it with me, but I know my dad wouldn't wager his wagon train." James LaVish turned to face Johanna. "I know my father, Ms. Remington, and I have to believe that Freddy Rotini pressured him into the wager and then cheated him."

"And I know Freddy!" Her mind was racing. She wasn't the argumentative type. Why was she suddenly so eager to defend Freddy in the middle of the night in a pouring rainstorm with an insulting man who had been hired because of nepotism? "Freddy would *never* cheat."

"Well, he did one time, and he cheated the wrong man. My dad could beat him in a minute—given the chance."

"If you're so sure, Mr. LaVish, why don't we set up another game of poker and let your father try to win the business back?" Johanna folded her arms across her chest.

"Another card game? You and I and a few of the crew are the only ones who know how my father lost the RIDE THE OREGON TRAIL WAGON TREK." James lowered his voice and gave her a wistful glance.

"Good Lord, an exhibition of that kind would humiliate Dad."

"I didn't say it had to be public."

Seeming to ignore her comment, James set a large pot on the counter, then began sorting vegetables into piles. "You're going to help me make stew. The crew and passengers will need it—campfire or not." He handed Johanna five onions and a large cleaver. "This poker game you suggested... I think Dad would agree to a rematch as long as it's private, and if I can observe Freddy closely during the game."

"I understand. You want to protect Charlie," she said quietly, but her attention was focused elsewhere. "Family can be i—important."

Onions. Her fingers curled around the rounded surface of the smallest specimen. Onions always made her cry, but not for the obvious reason. The rain, the flooding, the sense of emergency had been bad enough. The added odor of onions made the bitter memory complete.

She'd been alone with her mother chopping onions for soup that night so long ago in rural Missouri when the flood had washed away the bridge. The adolescent Joey had been left alone with her mother in labor and no one to help.

For more than fifteen years, she had avoided the smells, sights, and sounds that set off little flags in a corner of her mind where she'd thrust that painful memory and stored her feelings of guilt and inadequacy.

"You'll tell Freddy about the poker game, then?" James LaVish paused, his potato peeler held in midair.

Johanna lifted the knife, aimed at the small onion,

and brought the blade to rest against the paper-thin skin. Her hand was shaking badly. She paused, wordlessly put down the knife, and walked to the steps that led out of the chuck wagon.

Johanna needed fresh air and a glimpse of reality. In the clearing beyond, flashlights illuminated the muddy drama. The enormous wagon still rested on its side in the mud. It was obvious that Freddy Rotini had taken charge of the rescue operation with some help from the former wagon master. After conferring with Charlie Vishtek, Freddy began barking orders to the huddled forms behind him, all grasping thick ropes and digging their heels into the muck.

The wagon lifted and bucked, resisting the pressure of the ropes. The scenario could last well into the night, Johanna realized. Man battling nature's fury.

She'd been there before—as a tomboy in braids. That time, nature had won and changed her life forever.

Johanna swallowed hard as she turned her back on the scene and stepped back into the chuck wagon.

"Hey, I'm asking you a question." James LaVish's tone was impatient. "Will you talk to Mr. Rotini about this poker game?"

"Does he know that you and your father think he cheated?"

"My father's never actually accused Freddy . . . in so many words. In fact, don't mention this to my dad until I have a chance to talk to him alone." The cook shifted his weight from one foot to the other. "Will you tell Freddy?"

Johanna had the uneasy feeling that James LaVish had some personal grudge against Freddy and was using his father's misfortune as an excuse to strike back at the new wagon master.

"Okay. I'll mention it to Freddy tomorrow when the excitement dies down." Johanna picked up the knife. This journey had ripped open parts of her past and forced her to confront childhood memories both pleasant and painful. Perhaps it was time to face the most agonizing of her remembrances. She sliced neatly through the onion.

Freddy pulled off the hood of his rainslicker, stepped beneath the canvas canopy of the chuck wagon, and set his coffee cup down on the makeshift wooden counter. The rain had stopped, the wagons were secure, and his mouth tasted like mud.

"I could use a refill of—" The hoarseness of his own voice surprised him, but on a night like tonight, a person didn't take the time to catalog aches, pains, or fatigue. He cleared his throat forcefully. "Coffee, please."

"How about a bowl of hot stew this time, Mr. Wagon Master?"

The female voice was as hoarse as his, but the lilt of her words seemed vaguely familiar. Freddy looked at the slender form bending toward him. Her head seemed to be encased in some sort of bag. He squinted to clear his fatigue-blurred vision. "Johanna, is that you?"

"Of course, it's me. Someone offered me a stocking cap and I stuck my hair inside. I must look like Tugboat Annie but I had to stay warm. It's been a long night."

Light caught the side of her cheek. Her eyes were

large, luminous . . . and pleading. "Freddy, you better take this bowl. It's burning me."

He welcomed the heat from the metal campware against his numbed fingers. As the bowl passed between them, their hands touched. "You're cold," Johanna said softly before she placed her warm palms over Freddy's knuckles, sandwiching him between the hot metal of the bowl and the heat of her hands.

"I've been grabbing cups of coffee all night and never realized you were in there." Freddy was too tired to be astonished. Besides, astonishment seemed to be a regular occurrence for him when Johanna Remington was nearby.

"I'm not surprised. James LaVish had me out of sight in the shadows, chopping vegetables, making gallons of coffee, and doing dishes like a scullery maid. Not that I'm complaining," she added quickly. "Chef LaVish should be back anytime now. You better eat before the stew cools." Johanna removed her hands from the back of his and Freddy heard the rustle of silverware.

"Spoon or fork?" she asked. Something sputtered on the stove behind her, and muttering a quick apology, she turned to attend to it.

"Johanna, believe me. You don't look anything like Tugboat Annie," Freddy said, suddenly feeling the need to tell her. He was overwhelmed with pride at the way she had helped the cook. "And I'd prefer a spoon, please." He heard her laugh in response. She returned to the counter with the specified utensil.

"How's the cleanup going?" she asked, leaning over and watching while he devoured the fragrant concoction.

"We've got wagon number five mopped up. The

philosophers, including your former wagonmate, are a little bruised and shaken up. Great stew . . . it hits the spot. Anyway, the number five passengers are bedded down in the crew's wagon for now. No serious damage done to the contents." He gave her a brief rundown of each crisis they'd encountered during the night. "Thank God, the rain's finally stopped. The crew's ready to fall asleep on their feet."

"Is Poco all right?" There was a tinge of alarm in Johanna's voice.

"He's been sleeping safely in Tiffany's wagon most of the night. Right now, I've done everything I can do. What I'd really like is a good bath."

"Me, too." Johanna pulled the stocking cap from her head and shook her hair free. Reaching out, she lifted up the canopy and squinted toward the east. "It'll be daybreak in less than an hour. This might be my chance to sneak down to the river—"

"Not the river. The current's too fast. There's a stream nearby. It's probably swollen with rain, too, but it'd be safer, and it wouldn't be quite as muddy, either."

Freddy studied Johanna's slender form. Despite the velour top, mountain parka, and voluminous apron, she looked frail and vulnerable. "You'd better not bathe alone. It's too dangerous. I—I—uh—I'll come with you." He set the empty bowl on the counter.

"You'll bathe *with* me?" Johanna stared at Freddy's mud-caked face with disbelief.

"You'll have your privacy. You said it wouldn't be light for an hour or more. And I promise to be the perfect gentleman."

Johanna didn't want a perfect gentleman. She

wanted Freddy Rotini to understand that her voyage of self-discovery wasn't supposed to include an uninvited roommate and skinny-dipping. Why did he insist on rushing her? "First you move into my wagon, then you propose that we . . . get naked together and—"

Freddy moved around the counter and stepped through the door to the interior of the chuck wagon. "Right now I'm not proposing *anything* except washing this mud off and looking like two presentable human beings." His voice was an urgent whisper. "Have I ever done anything to make you feel uncomfortable?"

"Well—" Johanna couldn't begin to list the moments when Freddy's presence had unsettled her. They were too numerous. She did a quick visual inventory of their mud-splattered clothes and flesh. If she didn't wash her hair this morning, there wouldn't be a chance until nightfall. The thought was unpleasant. And the faint odor of onions lingered on her hands. "I—I do need a bath."

"Good. Then it's decided. I'll join you." Freddy reached around behind her to unfasten the apron strings.

He seemed to be taking care not to touch her with his damp slicker, but the coarse shadow of his beard brushed against her temple. Johanna heard her own sharp intake of breath. When Freddy moved back, she looked up into his dark gaze. Fatigue mingled with a faint glint of amusement in their depths.

"You seem pretty self-assured about this arrangement." She stepped past him, took the apron from his hand, and draped it over the proper hook on the back of the door.

"Me? Self-assured? No, it's just that I don't want you getting washed away in a flash flood without anyone watching." Freddy pushed a strand of hair back from her forehead with the gentleness of a lover.

"Do I understand you correctly?" Johanna moved away from his disturbing touch. "It's better that I get washed away in a flash flood while I have an *audience?*"

"An appreciative audience of one, Johanna."

Freddy balanced the lantern on a tree stump close beside the fast-running stream. "I've searched up and down the bank. This looks like the best spot so far . . . safety-wise. What do you think?"

Johanna stepped out of the semidarkness into the halo of light. "It's certainly secluded . . . but the water's moving pretty fast. We won't be able to venture out into the stream very far."

"That's the point. It's probably best if we stay in this pool right here. We won't have to fight the current and the water is cleaner." Freddy indicated an inlet where the water swirled in slow circles and lapped calmly against the bank. "We won't be washing mud off with mud."

He glanced over at his wagon mate. Despite the look of uncertainty on Johanna's face, her fingers were already moving down the front of her jacket.

Freddy followed suit. They undressed quickly in an awkward silence, each averting their gaze though they stood only a short distance apart. Both of them had brought a set of clean clothes, which they'd stuffed into a single backpack. As Freddy arranged the pack in the shrubbery beside the stream, he was very much aware of Johanna's steady breathing blending with his own.

"I'm ready," she said with a catch in her voice that made him turn.

Freddy tried to keep his eyes level with hers until they stepped down the bank to the edge of the water. Recalling his promise to act like a gentleman, he let her move ahead of him. The lantern cast a warm glow on her receding body. With an approving eye Freddy studied Johanna's graceful lines from the wild tumble of hair down the hollow of her back to the narrowing of her waist. Her hips flared gently into enticing curves that made his body react with unbearable swiftness.

She stepped into the shallow water caressing the bank and immediately discovered the steep drop-off concealed by the dark waters. "Arrrghhhh!" Johanna gasped, almost losing her grip on the bottle of shampoo she was clutching as she slipped down the incline and found herself thigh deep in a swirling eddy. Rather than retreat from the cold, she continued wading deeper with determined strides.

"Nnnn-uhhhhhh!" Freddy was quieter but no more articulate as his toes encountered the drop-off, and he slid down the dramatic incline, absorbing the shock of cold water that reached his knees. It had the same effect as a cold shower. His ardor abated. "Johanna, maybe it's better if we just get it over with in a hurry!"

"You mean... jump in headfirst? Go all the way under?" Johanna twisted around in time to see Freddy's large backlit frame break the gently swirling surface of the inlet and disappear. With a shrug she followed his example, her shout of youthful exuberance absorbed by the water.

Freddy surfaced first, then reached out to assist her. "It's d—deeper than I thought!" he gasped, treading water with steady strokes. "But it's still a lot safer than the river or moving farther out into the stream bed."

"The perfect swimming hole." After releasing the plastic shampoo bottle to float on the surface, she swept the damp strands of hair back from her face. "And it's fairly clear despite the heavy rain."

Freddy watched with amusement as Johanna Remington let out a whoop and swam in a frantic circle around him, shattering his last impression of her as a "staid schoolmarm."

"Oh, I almost forgot! I need to wash my hair," Johanna exclaimed, capturing the shampoo bottle and holding it up in the dim light. "I m—might need help. I don't think I can tread water and suds up at the same time."

"I'll steady you." Freddy reached beneath the surface of the water before he realized the implication of his words. His hands encountered the soft swell of her naked hips. Slowly he inched his fingers upward to grasp her by the waist.

Johanna shampooed her hair vigorously, leaning sideways to rinse, then squeezed some of the thick liquid into her palm. "You probably need a little of this, too," she said with a laugh as she dropped the bottle back in the water and lathered Freddy's mud-caked curls.

A series of sensations coursed through his body, defying the chilling effects of the stream. Freddy felt the languid movements of her long legs perilously close to the juncture of his thighs. Her calf touched his. Her glistening face and water-slicked shoulders were only inches away. As Johanna massaged the shampoo through his hair, her fingers moved toward the back of his head. He shuddered as her breasts brushed against his chest.

"I think it's time to rinse," Freddy said quickly, releasing his grip on her waist and ducking himself beneath the pool's surface. Underwater, he shook his hair clean of the suds and tried not to think of the feminine curves within his reach in the inky depths of the swimming hole.

He moved cautiously to the surface and brushed the water from his eyes. Johanna was swimming a short distance away. The first light of dawn was breaking in the distance, allowing Freddy the shaddowy vision of her body moving though the water with playful abandon.

"Feels good, doesn't it?" she cried out. "Swim a little. It's invigorating."

Invigorating? The thought of Johanna was rousing enough, but Freddy began to move through the water. The aches and stiffness brought on by the long night's work were forgotten as he stretched his limbs and adjusted to the temperature of the pool. After circling the inlet, he shifted to a crawl and headed toward her. In a few smooth strokes, Freddy was at her side.

"Joey," he called hoarsely, reaching out to pull her close. The ethereal hues of early dawn were mirrored in the water's surface, making the olive tone of her skin glow like moist satin. Reaching out, Freddy gently traced the shell of her ear until he encountered the smooth round contour of a pearl. Silently, he studied the soft rainbow of pastels reflected in the large, luminous pearl earrings that were ever-present. He felt a twinge of regret. He knew so little about her; had someone special given her these mementos? Freddy brushed his concern aside. He knew so little yet he sensed so much.

"You're beautiful, Joey. Have I told you that?"

Freddy rolled onto his back and gently pulled her lithe body atop his. The feel of her breasts pressing against his chest was sweet agony. Freddy extended his arms outward and together their bodies glided gracefully over the surface of the pink-hued pond.

Johanna's mouth parted, half in surprise, half in anticipation. She reacted with a flutter kick, which only made matters worse. The movement sent her skidding inches down his body until Freddy's arousal anchored her to him in a most intimate manner.

For a moment, her mind was flooded with memories of her teenage years in Missouri and skinny-dipping with Ronnie Buck, and then the images passed. The physical resemblance between Freddy and Ronnie was no longer blurred. As she gradually put the past behind her, the two men became separate entities, and their differences became more distinct.

Johanna realized she could no longer deny her feelings for Freddy. She tried to inch up slightly to avoid his disturbing pressure between her legs but her movements only served to heighten her arousal . . . and his.

Johanna saw the torment in Freddy's eyes and knew it reflected her own. Her arms moved around his back as her legs nestled snug against his thighs. She was filled with wanting and the need to be wanted.

"Freddy. My God, Freddy! All I meant to do was wash my hair—" she gasped. "I never intended to—Lord, I can't even make sense!"

"Don't explain," he said with a chuckle. "You washed your lips and can't do a thing with them, right?"

"Wrong," Johanna whispered before she closed her eyes and lowered her lips to meet his. The fierce flame spiraled within her as his mouth responded, possessing her with a surprising urgency.

She pulled away and rested her cheek against his. "I want you, Freddy," Johanna heard herself say aloud, and felt his body shudder in response. Her hands journeyed over the rise of his buttocks, pressing the steel of him tighter against her upper thighs.

Perhaps, Freddy thought, this watery bed had given him a false sense of buoyancy... making him believe his strong feelings for Johanna would compensate for his lack of honesty with her. While he ached for physical fulfillment, he also yearned to tell her the truth about his status as wagon master. How could he consider sharing her passion while wearing a false mask? The thought was distasteful.

"Not here. Not like this, Joey," he whispered with a near-groan beside her cheek. "There are elements to consider—like hypothermia... and the wrath of the other passengers. W—We have to get dressed and go back to the wagon. I told the crew we'd recheck the blocks this morning, get a few hours of rest, and depart at noon."

"Rest?" Johanna echoed. "We only have one sleeping bag."

"I'm very much aware of that... and you, all of you, right now."

While Johanna clutched his shoulders, Freddy did a lazy backstroke toward shore, pausing to allow her to retrieve the floating shampoo bottle. The gentle shades of sunrise caressed her body with an unearthly light that made him ache with need.

They had entered this pond expecting shallow waters and slipped into unexpected depths of desire. The phrase "in over one's head" was taking on new meaning as he stood up in the waist-high water and held her close.

"Do you realize," Freddy spoke close to her ear, "that I've seen you in lantern light, sunlight, and firelight? And now"—he touched her cheek with wet fingertips—"I'm seeing you in what I have to believe is love light, Johanna."

CHAPTER SIX

FIGHTING OFF A WAVE of weariness, Johanna spooned chicken salad onto her metal plate at lunch that same day.

"Pssst. Have you asked him yet?"

She lifted her eyes upward in search of the hoarse male whisper. James LaVish stood on the other side of the buffet lunch line, his eyes widened with anticipation.

"Ask who what?"

"P-O-K-E-R."

"Give me time," Johanna hissed.

"You've had eight hours."

"But I had to take a . . . bath." She lowered her gaze and picked up a large dill pickle. "And then there's this necessity called sleep."

"Necessity?" James leaned over the counter. "Sleep is a luxury for some of us."

"I'm aware of that." Johanna moved down the line,

shadowed by the oversized chef and his persistent remarks. She popped a green olive in her mouth and stuck two more on top of her salad. They stared back at her accusingly with pimiento pupils. She'd fallen asleep in the bedroll while Freddy left to check the blocks under the wagons with his crew. When she awoke, a fresh sprig of yellow blossoms rested on the empty pillow beside hers.

"For your information, Mr. LaVish, our wagon master didn't get any sleep at all last night or this morning."

"Neither did my father," the cook shot back. "Talk to Rotini today and report back to me tonight after the square dance. Now, hurry up. You're holding up the whole damn line."

Johanna could only stand openmouthed with surprise in front of the desserts.

James LaVish smiled graciously at the column of grumpy wagoneers waiting behind Johanna. "Let's be patient, folks," he said with a slight bow. "Ms. Remington spent the night fixing coffee and making stew for the crew. We all owe her our thanks." Turning, he quirked an eyebrow at Johanna. "She has her reasons for moving slowly today."

After spearing a brownie with her plastic fork, Johanna shook her head and went in search of shade. Her uneasy feeling about the cook's intentions was turning to suspicion.

"It looks sensational on you!" Coni Cameron backed up and moved the tiny mirror in her hands into a series of positions. "The light's fading. Are you sure you can see yourself?"

Johanna craned her neck. "I can see enough to

know I can't wear this dress to the square dance tonight."

"Why not? You look . . . devastating. That light pink flatters your skin color."

Johanna had seen coeds wearing dresses like this during spring and summer sessions. They always looked so carefree. Simple dress—simple life. But at the moment, her life wasn't simple. It was complicated by crazy new awakenings and by the presence of Freddy Rotini.

"You want to know why not?" She looked up at Coni. "Because this soft cotton blend clings to me—all over—except for the skirt, which swirls and sways every time I move. And it's practically strapless except for these tiny ties on the shoulders."

"Freddy is Italian, right? He'll love nibbling on your spaghetti straps."

Johanna smiled, then fidgeted with the three buttons Coni had left undone at the neckline. "It has buttons running from my north pole to my south pole, and you've left a lot of my northern and most of my southern hemisphere exposed. I'm warning you. I stop at my equator!"

"Afraid to show some latitude?" Coni responded with a laugh. "For heaven's sake, Johanna, stop being so prudish and leave those buttons undone. You're showing a lot less skin than some of the women in camp. And you've certainly got the figure for it."

"Too much figure in some places!" Johanna motioned for Coni to move the mirror up. "Take a closer look. I can't wear a bra under this fabric and the . . . uh, state of my emotions will be more than evident."

Do you think those pioneer women you've

studied all your life had time to put on a bra? Get into the spirit!"

"Flaunting myself is pioneer spirit?" Johanna shook her head and laughed. She tapped her sandaled foot on the ground beside the wagon. "Excuse me, but I think they're probably rolling over in their graves three times and putting a curse on my thesis."

As Coni moved the mirror downward, Johanna caught a glimpse of the full sweeping skirt, unbuttoned to mid-thigh. She was about to protest but something stopped her. The thought of Freddy's hands slipping through the seductive opening, his fingers lightly brushing the sensitive skin of her thighs . . .

"Uh, I thought you called this a simple sundress, Coni," she said absently.

"Some dress, huh? You'll discover it sort of grows on you," Coni responded with a laugh. "Come on, brush your hair and let me play with your makeup before Freddy and Poco return from the crew wagon and see you."

Johanna waited in the shadows until the hoedown music was in full swing and several couples were moving in complicated patterns around the campfire. After buttoning—then unbuttoning—the bodice of her dress in mute frustration, she stepped out into the flickering light of the camp to watch the colorful swirling figures.

No one will notice me here, Johanna thought as she tried to meld into the side of a wagon. She looked down at the soft pink fabric. Coni was right. It was a beautiful dress. But the thing seemed to take on a life of its own when it came in contact with Johanna's skin. The sensation was exciting, and she felt a surge of pride. Though she was nearing thirty, she'd kept her body in good shape.

But for some reason, Johanna didn't feel entirely comfortable about the fact that she'd found herself slipping into this masquerade with ease. Letting down her hair and unbuttoning the front of her tailored blouses were one thing, but borrowing clothes, applying makeup, and strutting behind the wagon seemed wanton. And all of the fantasies she'd entertained while waiting in the shadows and feeling the cool night breeze stroke her exposed flesh included Freddy.

Her heart was moving in syncopation with the music when she spotted Freddy approaching from the opposite side of the camp. She watched his white hat bobbing above the crowd as he threaded his way through the dancers and around the fire. When he moved close to the flickering flames, their fiery dance was reflected in the smooth white satin of his shirt, a flattering western style trimmed with purple piping. He stopped a short distance away.

"Johanna." Freddy took off his hat as he spoke her name. "I've been looking for you."

She could feel the heat of his gaze raking over the details of the dress. Freddy had never looked at her in such a bold, assessing manner before. Self-consciously, Johanna toyed with the buttons on the skirt.

"It's not mine," she explained. "This is one of Coni's dresses. She's a little shorter than I am . . . by a few inches, so naturally the hem is . . . well, the hem—"

"There isn't *any* hem in some places," Freddy observed in a calm, quiet voice that belied the surge of desire he was experiencing. The shadows between her breasts captured his attention and held him fascinated... until he saw the movement of the ebony waves of her hair against the smooth, flawless skin of her bare shoulders. And then he examined the subtle transformation in her face. Her eyes appeared larger, yet more mysterious. Her shaded cheekbones guided his eyes to her full sensuous mouth. Johanna's lips glistened with the same soft pink as her dress.

He'd come prepared to dance with a beautiful, entrancing woman in jeans. He'd found more flesh than he'd bargained for, more woman than he knew how to handle—because he was realizing he didn't truly know Johanna. Each time he attempted to insert her into any sort of mental category or to label her, she defied his expectations.

That first day, dressed in tailored outdoor wear, she looked like she'd stepped out of the pages of an L. L. Bean catalog *with pearls*. This morning, in the pink-hued water of dawn, she'd been playfully seductive, wearing nothing but her desire for him. Now, she looked like a fantasy come to life—warm, feminine, and incredibly seductive. Five days on the Oregon Trail and Johanna Remington was metamorphosing with each hour.

How was he going to carry on a serious conversation with her, to explain the way he'd been playing the role of wagon master without experience, when she looked so temptingly gift wrapped? When he was so eager to peel off the wrapping and demonstrate his attraction for her?

The music slowed. "Would you like to dance?" Johanna asked. She couldn't bear another moment of

Freddy's frank visual appraisal of her body. She was used to his open, easygoing manner, not these secretive smiles and penetrating stares.

"One dance," Freddy replied, reaching out for her hand, "and then, if you don't mind, we need to talk . . . seriously." There was nothing disapproving in the depths of his cocoa-brown eyes when his gaze met hers. Once again, she witnessed a fleeting glimpse of the melting vulnerability she'd seen the day they met.

They moved to the perimeter of the circle of slow-dancing couples before Johanna responded to his remark. "What do you mean? Why do we need to talk, Freddy?"

He took her in his arms and rested his cheek against her temple. "I might as well begin now." There was warmth in his tone. "There's so much I need to say. And if I can be frank, it would have been a lot easier for me to say these things if you *hadn't* worn that dress."

"What exactly do you need to tell me?" Johanna asked softly.

He drew back, loosening his embrace as he moved her in a slow, lazy circle. The clinging pink fabric outlined the swell of her breasts with enticing clarity. Freddy knew he was taking a chance by telling her the truth. Johanna was a warm, caring, intelligent woman. She'd spent hours in the chuck wagon the night before, performing menial kitchen tasks to assist the crew. Seeing her in this dress tonight, feeling her warmth against his chest as they danced, was a painful reminder of how much he had to lose.

"I'm an impostor, Johanna," he announced suddenly, forcing himself to look straight into her wide, startled eyes. "From the hat to the boots and everything in between. I'm not a wagon master." He felt his hand ball into a fist at her waist and his body tensed. "I'm a truck driver posing as something else. I haven't earned the right to lead this train—"

"Freddy—" Johanna put a finger to his lips and shook her head. "There's no need to do this to yourself. I know all about Charlie Vishtek and Reno and the poker game. I overheard you talking to Poco about it after the last square dance."

"That's just great, Johanna." With exaggerated force, he swirled her away from the other dancers. "It must have been a pretty impressive scene for a doctoral candidate to stumble upon. An impostor telling his problems to a half-pint Chihuahua. I'm surprised you ever spoke to me again—considering."

He stopped dancing and stared down at her, his eyes darkening with emotion. "Why have you pretended all this time?"

"Pretended what?"

"To respect me."

"I never pretended anything." Johanna jerked out of his embrace and turned away, walking quickly toward the shadows beyond the nearest wagon. She didn't look back. Hearing the pain in his voice was enough. She didn't want to see it reflected in his features.

"Johanna! Wait!" She felt Freddy's fingers close around her upper arm. She pulled away and continued walking.

"Where are you going?" he demanded.

"To the wagon... down to the river... back to Yale. I don't know." She whirled to face him. Moonlight illuminated the ragged torment in his features.

Handsome features. The pull of attraction was overwhelming. "I never had to pretend when it came to my feelings about you, and dammit, I resent your implying otherwise, Freddy."

"But in the beginning?"

Johanna looked down at the ground. "I'll be honest with you," she said after a few minutes. "At first, I felt rather smug. I was tempted to put your knowledge of the Oregon Trail to the test a few times. I even considered asking you to admit your novice status to all the passengers on the train."

"Smug, huh?" he said with a hoarse whisper. "Sounds more like priggish to me."

"I deserve that. Don't worry, my smug phase was short-lived—because I realized something important, Freddy. You're a master at making people feel at ease. I suspect that's an important trait for a man in your position."

He wondered if Johanna considered it an important trait for a man in any position.

"In some ways, we're all impostors . . . trying to be what people think we should be." She began walking through a grove of trees toward the river. "Maintaining an image. Stepping into the roles of people we admire for a moment. Why do you think people responded to your ad? They want a chance to feel like a pioneer for ten days."

He held a large branch aside and together they stepped onto a grassy knoll overlooking the moonlit waters.

"But the passengers are paying for the experience," Freddy protested. "They all know it's for a limited time. It's different for me, Johanna. I'm being forced to play wagon boss because Charlie Vishtek wasn't playing poker with a full deck that night. He'd been drinking." Turning slowly, Freddy reached out for her and ran his palms over the bare skin of her upper arms.

The movement didn't allay her fears. Could James LaVish be right? Had Freddy taken advantage of Charlie?

"You didn't have to accept the stakes, did you?" she asked. She had to find a way to bring up the cook's accusation of cheating—tactfully—if such a thing was possible.

"Accept the stakes? When Charlie said he was wagering a wagon train, I thought he was talking about a toy, a scale model of some kind. I accepted the wager thinking I was doing him a favor."

"But when you won, Freddy, and you found out the truth—"

"Charlie Vishtek is a proud man. Too proud, perhaps. I explained the misunderstanding, but he insisted. I accepted because I wanted to help him save face." Freddy moved his thumbs up and down over the smooth skin of her arms before he slipped his hands around Johanna's waist.

"I'm something of an enigma to the other truckers, Joey. 'Plato on Eighteen Wheels' they called me, because of my degree in philosophy. I might have a gypsy soul but I've never been much of a gambler, and I seldom drink. That night I was driving through Reno and something pulled at me. It reached out and drew me into the bar where I met Charlie. Who knows. Maybe I was due for a change."

Freddy released his hold on her waist and stepped away. He stood on the crest of the knoll, his back to her, as he stared at the water. "I leased my rig and went out and bought cowboy boots and the hat and new jeans, like an actor dressing for a part."

Without looking back at Johanna, he took off his hat and sat down on the grass. He bent one leg and perched the cowboy hat atop his knee.

She brushed aside all thoughts of James LaVish and his accusations of cheating. Perhaps if Freddy explained the circumstances, there'd be no need for a rematch. At the moment, she was more interested in Freddy's belief in himself as wagon master.

"You weren't acting last night when you took over the rescue operation to get wagon number five out of the mud. Your crew respects you." Johanna touched his shoulder. He looked up at her, then slowly lowered his knee and pulled her gently into his lap while mumbling something about not wanting grass stains on her dress.

"Maybe you're just searching," she suggested as she arranged the loose edges of the skirt modestly over her exposed thighs. With a sigh, she rested her head against his shoulder. "And maybe this adventure is part of that search?"

"Maybe? Lord, I swear you can read my mind sometimes."

"It isn't hard, Freddy. I feel the same way." With her fingertips, she touched his jaw, then moved her hand upward to caress his cheek. "Look at the dress and makeup I wore tonight. I feel like I'm playing a part, too . . . searching for the real me or all the parts that make me who I am. What do you think I'm trying to tell you by dressing like this?"

When he smiled, his features relaxed. "The same thing you tried to tell me this morning, Joey . . . that you want me. I was hesitant then."

Twisting his head, he kissed the palm that held his cheek so tenderly. His index finger traced the thin strap on her shoulder downward until the pad of his fingertip encountered the rise of her breast. He heard her sharp intake of breath.

"Joey," he whispered as his hand moved lower, to the shadowed valley between her breasts. "I wanted you to know the truth. Do you understand that I didn't want you to make love to a man in a mask?"

"Do you understand that I saw *behind* the mask? And that I liked what I saw? That I loved what I saw?"

Freddy punctuated her answer with the joyful response of his mouth on hers. It was a soft caress that teased and tantalized and tasted of promise. Johanna parted her lips with a moan. The pressure of his mouth on hers was spreading a liquid warmth through her limbs, immobilizing her.

Freddy traced the heart-shaped pattern of her upper lip until he felt it quiver beneath the sensitive tip of his tongue. He absorbed her sweet pleasured sounds with a series of languid kisses; then, whispering her name, he took her full bottom lip between his teeth and exerted the slightest of pressure.

Her fingers reached for the buttons on his shirt, unfastening them with blind detached movements until her hand was free to steal inside, to feel the warmth of his flesh and revel in the hard strength of corded muscles.

While he bent to kiss the soft shadows at her throat, Freddy ran a finger over the delicate bone buttons that remained fastened on the bodice of her dress, then returned to the top button. His fingers lingered there, gently coaxing the smooth oval disks, one by one, through a slip of fabric. Patiently, he parted the soft pink cloth, exposing her flesh to moonlight and to his impassioned gaze.

Lowering her farther into the cradle of his lap he bent his head and circled the hardened bud of one breast with his tongue before his mouth hovered, then closed over the aching peak.

His free hand grazed her hip and moved down the skirt of her dress until he encountered the contrast between the clinging jersey and the smooth warm flesh of Johanna's thigh. He felt her body tense as he raked his nails gently upward while with his lips he captured her mouth, savoring the sweet probing of her tongue against his.

Freddy paused for a moment to unbutton his cuffs and then shrugged out of his white satin shirt. "It's part of the mask," he whispered to Johanna. "I don't want it to come between us."

Johanna ran her tongue over her lips and tried to speak. Her own mouth felt swollen, throbbing with a sweet ache from the onslaught of his kisses.

"I love you, Freddy." She spoke the words against his lips.

"And I love you," he repeated, his mouth settling on the parted softness of her mouth, deliciously wet and willing, in a warmly ravaging kiss.

"Then please undress me, Freddy." It was a ragged entreaty. "I want to love you completely, here . . . now . . . in the moonlight."

He touched the strap on her shoulder, tugging on one of the loose ends until the bow untangled with a whisper-soft rustle that thrilled him. He paid equal attention to the other shoulder and the dress fell away.

Moments later, they lay naked on the cool grass, legs and arms entwined as they curved into the warmth of each other's bodies, their senses lulled by the rushing water and awakened by the newness of discovery.

He caressed her, kissed her, touched her with a gentleness that made her want to weep with emotion. She gave herself up to the mastery of his loving as he paid homage to her with his hands and lips, whispering his love for every part of her.

Unwilling to remain passive, Johanna trailed her fingertips over the broad expanse of Freddy's smooth chest to the taut muscles of his midriff. The moonlight through the trees created dappled patterns of silver and shadow across his upper body.

She touched the silvered treasures first, delighting in the masculine beauty and corded strength she found beneath her fingertips. Then slowly she sought the bounty hidden in shadow. She heard him moan softly as her fingers journeyed over his abdomen and touched the column of smooth satin rising from a triangle of mutinous curls. Her fingers curled around him possessively.

Frantic with wanting, Freddy spread kisses along her slender throat. He was lost in the fragrance of her silky black waves, the delightful sensations her touch induced in him, and his own anxious desire to awaken all of her senses to him. His upper torso held her pinioned to the ground. Her breath was ragged against his cheek as Freddy's hands trailed back down her body to the apex of her thighs, the gentle swell between her legs. His own control was dissolving as he explored the silky velvet softness, testing her readiness.

Johanna clutched and released the grass beneath her fingertips. She was shaking, straining against the hunger of delayed excitement.

He moved his body over hers, hovering above her beauty, seeing the hazy torment of need in her eyes. A strong breeze rustled through the trees, leaving her shoulders and breasts bathed in a shimmering silver-white glow. Freddy wanted to remember the moment forever—Johanna's blanket of ebony waves spreading over the grass, her expression soft and willing as her hips rose up to meet his first thrust, to join them as one.

Freddy heard himself moan as her feminine warmth surrounded him, inch by agonizing inch, and the rest of the world fell away. He captured her quicksand cries with his lips as their bodies fused in a soaring rhythm that matched their spiraling need. His eyes grew moist at the beauty of her giving.

Johanna felt her mouth go dry as she let the last vestige of control die and the pleasure peaked within her. Waves of ecstasy drowned her in a chaotic network of shivers that made Johanna pray the tumultuous sensations would end, yet never end. Never.

When he felt her contract convulsively around him, Freddy allowed himself the sweet pleasure of his own release. Contentment flooded his limbs as he gathered Johanna in his arms and tunneled his fingers through the rich wealth of her hair.

"Freddy—" she spoke his name in a thready whisper that became a warm rush of air against his shoulder.

"Hmmm?" Freddy shifted in their embrace.

"I understand now."

He opened one eye and peered into her smoldering gaze. "What? You've had a revelation? If it has anything to do with Manifest Destiny, I don't want to hear it. This isn't the time—"

"No," she responded with a throaty chuckle. Lifting her hand upward, she caressed his cheek with her palm. "I just want to say, you look wonderful in love light."

They entered the camp arm in arm. A dozen couples were swirling to Charlie Vishtek's square dancing calls. The campfire had burned down to a small flickering blaze and the younger children had been tucked into sleeping bags and wagon bunks.

"Good timing," Freddy whispered to Johanna. "I believe this is the final dance. I'm scheduled to make a little speech." He looked down at the crumpled white cowboy hat in his hand.

"I'm sorry—" her voice faltered.

"No, it wasn't your fault. We both rolled on that poor hat at one time or another. It's a small price to pay for the pleasure we shared tonight."

Johanna ran a finger along the grass-stained brim. The hat looked hopeless.

"Why don't you hold this for me," Freddy suggested. "Wearing a crumpled, dirty hat won't help my image as a dynamic wagon master."

"That reminds me." Johanna swallowed as she spotted James LaVish across the camp. "There's a message I was supposed to pass on to you."

The music ended and Charlie Vishtek thanked the band.

"About what?" Freddy smiled down at her as he ran his fingers through the shock of hair that hung over his forehead. "What is it? You look a little pale."

"Last night, when I was working with Chef LaVish in the chuck wagon, we got into a heated discussion about your leadership and—"

"LaVish has always held a grudge."

"Freddy, he thinks you cheated."

"What?"

"The cook thinks you cheated his father out of the wagon train. I know the truth because you told me tonight, but he doesn't know—"

"Calm down," Freddy urged her. "I'll just talk to him and explain things."

"That might work." Johanna swallowed hard. "But in my anger, I sort of suggested a rematch—to give Charlie a chance to win the wagon train back from you."

Freddy looked up at the makeshift stage as he tried to absorb her words. One half of his brain was running through tomorrow's activities and the change in course dictated by the storm. He'd be speaking to the crowd in a matter of seconds. "Good Lord, Johanna. This is hardly the time to make bad jokes."

"Freddy." Johanna touched his sleeve. "It isn't a joke. Mr. LaVish wants an answer from you tonight!"

CHAPTER SEVEN

"HIGH NOON TOMORROW, Mr. Rotini?"

"Agreed." Freddy nodded to the taller and fuller of the two shadowy figures standing outside his wagon an hour later. "I wish you'd reconsider. This is all a misunderstanding. I thought Charlie was wagering a toy—"

"A toy?" James LaVish put an arm protectively around his father's shoulder. "Does this operation look like child's play? The RIDE THE OREGON TRAIL WAGON TREK was the pride of my father's existence."

"After I los' the used car bus'ness, that is." Charlie shrugged. "I still don't understan' all this fuss about a rematch . . ."

"Let me handle this, Dad." James cleared his throat forcefully. "Since the train'll be passing close to a town or two in the morning, we can send a crew member out to buy a new deck of cards, Mr. Rotini."

Freddy folded his arms across his chest. Charlie,

the same man who kept the passengers enraptured with his talent for storytelling, had barely spoken. He looked oddly sad each time he glanced up to meet Freddy's gaze. Since the night of the storm, a mutual bond of respect had formed between them. Was he being forced in this attempt to win the wagon train back? Freddy wondered.

"I'll officiate, of course," the cook concluded with a self-satisfied smile. "We'll discuss the specifics . . . at *high noon*. Come on, Dad. You'll need your sleep."

Vishtek and LaVish, father and son, left as Freddy reached up to tip a hat that wasn't there. After a quick trip to the crew wagon, he stepped out of his boots and climbed into the back of the wagon.

Johanna was huddled in a corner dressed in her velour jogging outfit and reading a pioneer journal aloud to Poco. She closed the book and watched while Freddy began to undress in silence.

"Are you going through with the game?"

"High noon tomorrow."

"High noon? Isn't that a bit dramatic?"

"Cinematic. Comedic. You name it. I'm not looking forward to this." Freddy took off his satin shirt and blue jeans and began layering his body with sweat pants and shirts, and extra socks.

Johanna gave him a quizzical look before she began rolling out the sleeping bag and fluffing up the pillows. Freddy's bedroll was still too wet to use so they'd be sharing close quarters tonight. "I'm sorry I suggested the rematch, Freddy. I hope you're not upset with me."

He knelt on the bedroll beside her. "Frankly, I'd like to ring your beautiful neck"—he leaned forward, brushing his lips against her throat—"with kisses."

"I don't understand," Johanna stammered. "You might lose the wagon train tomorrow . . . because of something I said to James LaVish."

"Don't you see? I'm relieved to know the truth. I couldn't figure out this grudge thing until now, and it bothered me a bit. I like to know where I stand with people." Freddy ran a hand through his hair. "It's refreshing to know that LaVish thinks I'm a card shark preying on drunks and that it's nothing personal.

"I didn't cheat, Johanna. I've only played poker for money a few times. I wouldn't know *how* to cheat. In fact, I was hoping we could get a little practice in tonight." He pulled a deck of cards out of the pocket of his sweat pants. "I borrowed a deck from the crew. Do you play?"

"Not much. I played bridge all through college. Uhhh, actually when I was very young, I played . . . strip poker one time." Johanna swallowed hard as she recalled a Sunday afternoon in Ronnie Buck Ferguson's barn. Were his words responsible for stirring these memories?

"I told you former tomboys were always interesting." Freddy tapped a finger against the top of the deck.

"But the rules were pretty lax."

"They usually are—depending on who's playing. Did you win, lose, or what?"

"I lost, Freddy, but that was a lifetime ago. It's not very important." She sat cross-legged on the sleeping bag, holding Poco in her arms.

"I didn't mean to pry." Freddy settled on the bedroll, across from her. "I was just wondering what my odds are tonight . . . with you." He shuffled the cards with a loud snap and looked up at her with dark mischievous eyes.

"We're going to play strip poker? Here—in the wagon?"

"Want me to cut the deck?"

"Is that why you put on the extra socks and pants and—you *are* a cheat, Freddy Rotini!"

Poco growled and bared his teeth at Freddy.

"What is this—two against one? Guilty until proven innocent?" Freddy shook his head and laughed while he cut the deck. "Want me to deal? I really appreciate your helping me get some practice, Johanna."

Without waiting for her answer, Freddy dealt five cards to each side of the bedroll.

Disarmed by his take-charge approach, she set the squirming Poco in her lap with his rubber hamburger, picked up the cards, and studied her fate.

"Tell me the truth. Do you want to win or lose tomorrow?" she asked, looking up from her disastrous hand.

"I want to talk Charlie out of the rematch and offer him a partnership," Freddy answered without hesitation.

"That's really considerate of you, Freddy." Johanna was overwhelmed.

"But tonight"—he arranged the cards in his hand with a sly smile—"I'd love to beat the pants off you, Joey . . . and eventually I'd like to win that Ivy League heart of yours."

"The perfect hanging tree," Freddy muttered to Johanna as he looked at the card table and the two chairs set up under the large cottonwood in the field beside the wagon train's nooning spot. "How convenient. If I lose, Charlie and James can sit in the shade and toast their good fortune. If I win, they can make a noose—"

"There won't even *be* a game once you offer Charlie a partnership." She laced her fingers through his. "Good luck, break a leg, wagon ho, and all that."

Freddy pulled her into his arms and kissed her tenderly. "I only hope I'm as lucky as I was last night."

"Cheat," Johanna whispered beneath her breath. "I'm on kitchen duty for the next hour. I'll be anxious to hear."

"I don't understand. You agree with James? You want to turn down my offer to make you a partner, Charlie?" Freddy looked across the table at the grizzled old man. "I want to hear the answer straight from you, not your son."

"But I have an interest in my father's affairs," James protested.

"Your answer, Charlie?"

The former wagon master looked at his son, then back at Freddy. His expression was one of uncertainty. "Perhaps we should let the cards decide things t'day."

"What do you wager, Mr. Rotini?" the cook asked tersely.

"I wager the full ownership of the RIDE THE OREGON TRAIL WAGON TREK."

"Fine." James recited a long list of rules from a sheet of hand-scrawled notes. ". . . best of three hands is the winner, deuces are wild . . . Are we in agreement, gentlemen?"

"Wait," Freddy interjected. "In the original match, I wagered three hundred dollars. If this is a rematch, we both need to have something at stake."

"I ain't got no three hun'erd dollars," Charlie said quietly. He turned to James. "Son, I don't feel comfortable about this. I got a good thing here, being lead driver for Freddy. I'm happy."

"Dad, I'm just looking out for your interests."

Charlie glared defiantly at his son for a moment, then squared his shoulders and held his chin up. "I'll wager my pride!"

"Come on, Dad, pride isn't something you can wager."

"The hell it ain't! Pride is what helped me run this outfit fer five years. You seem to want to take over all my affairs, son. You want me to sit 'round like an ol' woman, a useless ol' woman while you run the show!" Charlie jumped up from his chair, his eyes darting fiercely around. He stalked toward a nearby clothesline strung between two of the wagons and jerked an oversized calico Mother Hubbard off the line.

"Dad! What are you doing?" James cried, rushing around the table. "Calm down and let me handle this."

"Stay out of my bus'ness, Jimbo. You're always so concerned about appearances." The older man walked past his son and sat down in the chair opposite Freddy. "If I lose," Charlie announced in a strangled voice as he gave the formless smock crumpled in his hand an extra shake, "I'll wear this here dress for the rest a' the ride!"

* * *

"Believe me, Charlie, I'd rather have lost!" Freddy bent his head.

Charlie bolted to his feet, grabbing a handful of calico from the edge of the table.

"No, Dad. For heaven's sake, you don't have to—" James LaVish pleaded loudly with his father.

"Shaddup! I said I'd wear it and I'm a man who keeps his word!" Charlie pounded a fist on the card table.

Freddy ran his fingers through his hair and found himself staring at the full house he'd just laid on the table. "Forget the game! What does a game of chance have to do with a man's livelihood? My offer still stands, Charlie—a partnership in the business. We can do it together."

"Gol durn thing." Charlie studied the dress with a puzzled expression. "I can't tell what's front and back—"

"Don't you dare put that dress on," James hissed. "We have the family name to protect."

Charlie pushed his hat back on his head and stared up at his son. "The fam'ly name, you say? Ain't you the one t' talk. You had to fancy it up fer cookin' school."

"We've been through this. Vishtek sounded too much like 'fish stick,' Dad. For the sake of both our names, I'm begging you not to put that dress on. Did you hear what Freddy said? He's still offering you that partnership."

"The one you had me refuse? You're the one that wanted me to play this fool game . . . and I never once accused Freddy of cheatin'. That was your concoction!" Charlie pulled the fabric over his head, and let the voluminous sheet of calico cascade down to his boot tops. "Right now, I've had it with the both of ya. Good day. I'm a workin' man. I have to grab some grub and tend to my chores as lead driver."

Chef Jimbo Vishtek? Freddy kept his elbows on the table and formed a steeple with his fingers to hide his embarrassed smile while James sat down. From the corner of his eye, Freddy saw Johanna approaching.

"Where's Charlie? What happened?" she asked quietly.

"Freddy cheated my father out of his pride." James LaVish glowered at both of them. He began slapping the cards back into a deck.

"You watched me every minute, James. And you know damn well I didn't cheat," Freddy insisted. "It was a new deck. I won fair and square, and even then I gave Charlie another chance to accept my original offer."

"Fair and square? A full house three times in a row?" The cook cocked an eyebrow and pointed a finger across the table. "I don't know how you did it, Rotini, but you shamed my father."

"But no one on the wagon train has to know," Johanna reasoned. "Your dad remains lead driver until he decides to accept Freddy's offer, right?"

"How many lead drivers have you seen that are forced to wear a dress?" James shot back.

"I'm not forcing him to wear that getup!" Freddy stood up abruptly, shaking the table and knocking over his chair. He pointed a finger at the cook. "I didn't want to have to tell you this, LaVish, but your father was drinking the night I beat him in Reno. And you heard him admit I didn't cheat him then."

"Wear a dress?" Johanna threw up her hands. "Would someone explain? What are you two talking about?"

"You took advantage of a drunk?" James spoke through clenched teeth.

Freddy drummed his fingers on the table. "I will admit . . . that I had been drinking a bit myself that night. If I had wagered my rig and lost it, would you accuse Charlie of taking advantage of me?"

"Don't confuse the issue." James LaVish rose slowly from his chair. He leaned forward across the table, his finger aimed at Freddy. "If I were you, Rotini"—his tone was ominous—"I'd sleep with one eye open."

The chef sauntered away. Freddy began to fold up the card table and chairs with Johanna's help.

She'd never meant the rematch to end in threats or with the former wagon master being forced to dress in drag. "Couldn't you have cheated—just a little—just to let Charlie win?"

"You can't really cheat in five-card stud." Freddy shrugged. "I told you about my sister winning all that money on the slot machines. It's genetic. I must have inherited the Rotini charm."

Johanna glanced up at his handsome features. "I can assure you some of that charm has nothing to do with cards, Freddy," she whispered.

"Beautiful, isn't it?" Johanna asked Coni as they stood at the base of Chimney Rock, staring upward in awe at the inverted funnel of clay and sandstone. Fellow passengers were moving up and down the nature trail that led to the base. Mr. Prescott set his tripod and camera up while several other photographers from the wagon train made suggestions about angles and f-stops. One of the young women from the singles' wagon sat sketching.

"Beautiful might be an understatement." Coni slapped dust off her jeans absently. "Freddy's clay model didn't do it justice in yesterday's lesson. But he sure had the kids worked up about visiting the site today. The man's a born teacher."

"That he is," Johanna agreed with a soft laugh.

"Do I detect a double meaning in your response?" Coni folded her arms across her chest and raised an eyebrow.

"Let's just say that Freddy has helped me to see a few things about myself more clearly in the past few days, Coni." Johanna made a circle in the hard ground with the toe of her boot.

"I wish you'd stop speaking in secret code, but then what can I expect? Love does that to people."

"Love?" Johanna stuck her hands in the back pockets of her jeans and tried to act nonchalant. "Isn't that a little presumptuous?"

"First of all, you forget we're staying in the wagon next to yours."

"Coni!" Johanna felt a warm blush start at the base of her throat.

"Secondly, you two can't keep your hands off each other. And look at you. There're four buttons undone on that blouse today. By the end of the trip you'll be—"

"That's enough! I get the picture." Johanna feigned surprise. "You were the one who told me to do some changing, to loosen up. One less button unfastened hardly makes me immodest."

"Come on, I'm joking. And speaking of change, the camp is buzzing with rumors about Charlie Vishtek, the lead driver. He's a . . . hmmm . . . been wearing a dress. My sons asked me and my husband quite a few questions last night. You know kids. They'd heard the word *transvestite* from an older boy and we were put on the spot."

"What did you tell them?"

Coni shrugged. "My husband's an expert in medieval history so he tried to explain how it was common for men, even kings and warriors, to wear tunics."

"I hope the boys bought Donald's explanation."

"No chance. I doubt if Charlie Vishtek will reach superhero proportion in their eyes during this trip. Now Freddy"— Coni put a hand over her heart—"is another matter."

"Superhero material, huh?"

"Oh yeah. Of course, the adults on this train may not see it that way." Coni followed Johanna's meandering steps near the base of the rock formation. "There's been a lot of ugly talk, Johanna. Rumor has it that Freddy Rotini is forcing that old man to wear the Mother Hubbard as some form of public humiliation. I found that hard to believe, but the cook and other members of the crew have confirmed it."

"But it's not true." Johanna explained the poker game as briefly as she could.

"Oh Lord, Freddy must feel awful." Coni shook her head. "Isn't there anything he can do? Charlie looks so pitiful . . . And that calico print does nothing for his figure."

Coni's laugh was infectious. Johanna found herself

joining in. "You have to understand. I think the problem is between Charlie and his son. I want to stay out of this. Remember how you told me this was a vacation, and we shouldn't gossip or concern ourselves with what other people on the wagon train do?"

"Johanna." Coni slapped her gently on the shoulder. "That was before the lead driver put on Olivia Prescott's dress!"

"I'm curious. What other rumors should I know about?"

Before Coni could answer, there was a plaintive cry for "Mom" in the distance. "Gotta go. From the sound of that, I'm wanted for something. It's not fair to leave this rock formation alone with my two kids for more than five minutes. They're armed with laser guns today."

"Don't worry," Johanna called after her departing friend as Coni hurried away, "this rock has been shot at, carved, chipped, clawed, and no doubt struck by lightning."

"You don't know my kids," Coni called back. "They give erosion a run for its money."

"Do you think this is wise—escaping by horseback to Chimney Rock to watch the sunset?" Johanna leaned back against Freddy's chest with a sigh.

"I had to get away from those accusing stares." Freddy took a deep breath. "I think James is spreading lies about me, and some of the formerly loyal passengers seem to believe him. People keep asking me to let Charlie take the dress off."

He touched a hand to her cheek and Johanna reached up to press it closer. The sunset was unfolding with scarlet splendor against the western sky, silhouetting the sandstone spire.

"Besides, I wanted to be alone with you," Freddy added. "The wagon camp isn't the most private of places. These past few days, I've had the powerful urge to reach out and touch you every time I see you."

His hand moved down her shoulder to the exposed skin on her upper chest.

"If you could carve a lasting impression on Chimney Rock, what would it be, Joey?" Freddy asked softly.

"I wouldn't think of touching a fingernail to it," Johanna replied. "I've read all the journals." She felt Freddy's fingertips stroke the cleft between her breasts. "It was such an impressive milestone that some pioneers wrote poetry about it, sketched it, painted it, and some scrambled up the rock more than a century ago to carve their names and destinations in stone. It's like the world's largest journal . . . even though the words have long since disappeared."

"So you have nothing to add?"

The last scarlet cloud of sunset lingered on the horizon. With deft movements, his fingers unfastened the remaining buttons on her blouse.

"I have nothing to add." Johanna inhaled sharply. "My own goals seem paltry in comparison. What about you, Freddy?"

With a quick rearrangement of limbs, he moved beside her, brushing the fabric of her blouse away from her flesh. He skimmed his thumb over the pebble-hard peak of one breast, then paused to cup the feminine fullness in his palm.

"I'm afraid that what I have to say isn't very original. But I believe it could be lasting."

With a smile, Freddy dragged his finger over her breast in a series of vertical and horizontal gestures, creating fiery sensations that made Johanna lean back on his shoulder for support.

"I take it I'm supposed to represent Chimney Rock?" she ventured.

"Uh-huh. But a far far lovelier version of it."

"And if I may ask, pilgrim, what are you inscribing?"

"Three words: I love you," Freddy whispered. "There wasn't room to say everything so I'll have to find another means to express it all."

"By all means—do." Johanna gasped as his mouth descended over her breast and her fingers entwined in his hair.

The camp was suspiciously quiet when they returned long after sundown. The light of the campfire blazed with eerie ferocity, illuminating the scowls and frowns of the crew members and passengers gathered around.

"Everything all right here?" Freddy dismounted, then turned to assist Johanna. "Charlie? James? Josh? What's going on?"

"There's been a theft, Freddy." Josh stood up and fingered his hat nervously.

"Really? What's missing?"

Josh turned as if on cue and looked at James LaVish. The cook stood and walked slowly toward Freddy and Johanna. "The lingonberries we bought for tomorrow morning's breakfast crêpes are missing, Mr. Rotini."

"Lingonberries? Why does everyone look so glum-faced over a few pints of berries?"

"And how did you happen to know it was a few pints, sir?" James LaVish confronted Freddy.

"Just a guess, James. Berries are usually sold in pints."

A murmur arose from the crowd seated around the campfire.

Freddy shifted his weight from foot to foot, feeling uneasy. The situation had setup written all over it. "Look, James, I'm sorry about the loss, but maybe you can substitute something else—"

"The menu calls for lingonberries. No one sleeps tonight until we find the thief and deal with him properly." James walked slowly around the campfire as he spoke, eyeing the passengers and crew members.

How did a wagon master deal properly with a lingonberry thief? Freddy pondered. Brand the culprit with a hot crêpe pan?

Freddy sat down on an upturned orange crate and Johanna sat close by. She surveyed the familiar faces in the circle, feeling uneasy. Her nails dug into her palms as she recalled the chef's anger following the poker game. The rematch had been her idea. By interfering in Freddy's affairs, had she brought about this confrontation?

"You know," Freddy declared, "there might be a simple explanation. A wild or domestic animal could have snuck into your food supply—a raccoon or something like that." He looked at the silent group. The hairs on the back of his neck stood up. "Did anyone see anything unusual going on?"

"In all my years," a mule skinner declared,

"there's never been a single varmint invade our food supply. I suspect it might be a low-life human with a cravin' for them lingonberries."

"Now, Hank, don't jump to conclusions," Charlie chastised as he picked sullenly at a spot on his dress. "No one's seen nothing pos'tive."

Professor Harold Billings stood up and straightened his glasses. "After hearing Hank mention low-life, I feel the need to add a word. I, too, have been the victim of a theft. I arrived from the East Coast with Johanna Remington as my wagon mate"—Harold shot an icy glance toward Freddy and Johanna—"and within two days, *Romeo* Rotini—a man whose *dog* knows more about the Oregon Trail than *he* does—forced me out of wagon number ten so he could parlay with that—that harlot of the plains!"

"Harold, you chose to leave the wagon." Johanna's angry rebuttal was lost in the incessant buzz of the crowd and the vociferous grumblings of the crew.

"And another thing!" Harold held up a hand as if to hush the murmurings. "Rotini was the last person to come near the philosophers' wagon the night of the storm. He tightened the canvas after asking us if we were comfortable." Harold lowered his voice to a conspiratorial whisper. "*Were we comfortable?* Ha! Hours later, the wagon was on its side in the mud, and only through determination and a little luck, did we, the occupants, escape a cruel death!"

"You were lucky to escape, Professor Billings." James LaVish sauntered back into the firelight. "My father was less fortunate. Challenged to a game of poker with Freddy Rotini a year ago, he lost his wagon train. Then yesterday, Rotini demanded a rematch and stripped Dad of what dignity was left him." LaVish pointed to Charlie. "My father is being forced to wear a dress until we reach our destination."

Members of the crew hissed and booed, then joined in, drowning out Charlie's protestations.

"We signed up for this trip thinking Charlie Vishtek was going to be wagon master!"

"We never had trouble till that Rotini fella took over."

Freddy rose to his full height and waited for silence. "All I want to say is that I've offered Charlie Vishtek partnership in the wagon train. His son didn't want him to accept it, but if Charlie's willing, I would gladly agree to another game of cards."

"So you can force him to wear the matching calico bonnet?" LaVish lashed out.

Freddy waited until the crowd quieted. He noted that most of the heckling was from crew members. Many of the passengers looked bewildered. "You're my guests," Freddy continued in a gentle but commanding voice, "and I want you to enjoy your trip. I'm sorry that you've been exposed to the rantings and accusations of James LaVish and Harold Billings. I only hope that you'll remember the lessons I've given your children and the way I've treated each of you on a one-to-one basis."

No one spoke. Freddy rubbed his palms together. "Maybe it would be best if we all got some sleep. This misunderstanding started with the lingonberries. Let's hope the guilty party will have second thoughts and come forward in the morning."

At that moment, Poco walked into the circle of the

campfire, his head hung low. He'd become something of a mascot to the passengers in the past week. People smiled and urged the dog their way with snapping fingers and coaxing sounds.

Poco walked straight to James LaVish and pawed the ground. With a groan, the cook bent over to pick up the Chihuahua. A communal gasp was heard as a telltale color became evident around the small dog's snout.

James looked at Poco, sniffed for a moment, then fixed his gaze at Freddy and Johanna. "The wagon master's dog has . . . lingonberry breath," he said in a low, steely voice.

"We could mutiny."

Freddy heard the murmur and turned in the direction of the crew. Their expressions were menacing, and belligerent, and the situation was volatile.

"Mutiny." Other voices from the crew section joined until the single word became a chant.

"We want Freddy!"

"We should all decide!"

Young and old, the passengers voiced their own protest.

"Okay, people. Let's be fair." James LaVish clapped his hands. "We'll vote to see who'll lead the wagon train! Rotini or Vishtek!"

Fair? Freddy almost choked. Perhaps this was to be the biggest test of his leadership on this journey. He felt Johanna's fingers lace through his and turned to smile at her. "From now on, I limit myself to strip poker . . . with you," he said with a whisper before he walked out to the center of the circle and stood beside the campfire.

"If I might say something before you hold this impromptu election?" Freddy held up his hands until the group grew silent. "I've enjoyed working with you and getting to know each of you. I grew up in a family of seven children and that taught me something about living in the real world. It taught me tolerance and patience. I hope that I'm not quick to judge others. I hope that I understand the nature of love."

Freddy glanced at Johanna's upturned face and saw tears glistening in her eyes. He looked down, then continued to speak. "Growing up in a large family also taught me something about harmony. For there to be harmony in a group, each member has to feel at peace with themselves. Now it's obvious that some of you are unhappy with my performance as your leader. I'm not going to argue with you about specifics."

A murmur went through the crowd. "If I were to insist on completing this trip as your wagon master, it would bring more disharmony to all of you. I'm hearing talk of a mutiny . . . and I don't want that. I don't want an impasse either. So tomorrow morning, I'll stay behind with my own wagon and team, and let the rest of you go on ahead under the leadership of Charlie Vishtek. I'll follow along in two days and discuss ownership of the RIDE THE OREGON TRAIL WAGON TREK with Charlie in private at an appropriate time."

Freddy looked at the many faces staring back at him. They reflected a myriad of emotions. When his gaze settled on Johanna, he felt an ache in his chest.

"No one will remain behind with me. It'd be unfair and possibly dangerous," he announced quietly. "I hope one of you will allow Johanna Remington to move into your wagon for the remainder of her journey."

CHAPTER EIGHT

JOHANNA'S MIND WHIRLED with the impact of Freddy's words. In front of a few dozen witnesses, he had told her this would be their last night together, that he'd chose to stay behind without her. What had he said about fairness and danger?

In her excitement she'd risen to her feet with the crowd. Now she felt wobbly with disbelief. Using her fingertips, she felt behind her for the rough texture of the orange crate and sat down slowly. Passengers from the train were gathering around Freddy, talking excitedly, a few reaching out to touch him as they wished him luck on the lonely path he had chosen.

A scenario played out in Johanna's mind. She would board the plane for the East Coast with Harold Billings in four days and resume her doctoral studies in a few weeks. *Dr. Johanna Remington*. The title sounded hollow, empty, devoid of fulfillment.

Hadn't she learned anything from her experience

with Ronnie Buck Ferguson so many years ago? What a fool she'd been to build fantasies in the sky, featuring Freddy Rotini as the dream prince who would magically make her life meaningful. She felt hot tears on her cheeks before she realized she was crying.

"Come on, I'll walk you back to your wagon." Coni Cameron's voice filtered through the pounding in Johanna's ears. Blindly, she accepted the elbow offered her and quickly tried to dry her eyes with the sleeve of her shirt.

"What are you going to do, Johanna?" Coni asked when they reached the wagon site. "Complete the journey with the rest of us or stay behind with Freddy?"

"I'm not sure. I think the wagon master made it rather clear that he wanted to be a—alone." Her voice cracked and Johanna felt fresh tears gather in her eyes. Coni's arms moved around her in a gentle embrace.

"Talk to him, honey," Coni urged. "Freddy was put on the spot tonight. He might not even know his own mind at the moment. Give him time to think about it and talk. All right?"

"I'm fine," Johanna murmured.

"In the meantime, can I ask you a stupid question?" Coni pulled back and looked into Johanna's eyes. "Just what the hell is a lingonberry, anyhow?"

Freddy slipped out of his boots and entered wagon number ten with trepidation. He'd pictured Johanna wrapped snugly in the sleeping bag and envisioned himself explaining the situation to her while she lay sleepily warm and naked in his arms. Instead he found her sitting on the floor of the wagon with her back to him, working busily at some unseen chore.

"Johanna?"

She laid something metal on the floor and turned to face him. In the soft glow of lantern light, he could see a faint puffy redness about her eyes and the slight quiver of her lower lip as she opened her mouth to speak. No sound came forth, which made his heart wrench even more.

Kneeling beside her, he gathered her in his arms and kissed the ebony hair at her temple. "I'm sorry," Freddy whispered in a voice hoarse with the pain of uncertainty. "It must have been terrible for you, watching from the sidelines while I stammered my way out of a mutiny, then let both of us be publicly accused of less than honorable behavior by Harold Billings. And now—"

His gaze was drawn downward by the glint of light on a butter knife. He was even more distracted when he saw the "chore" Johanna had been working on when he entered the wagon. His clay model of Chimney Rock—the one he'd used in yesterday's history lesson for the children—lay on the floor. On the large base of the rock formation, Johanna had neatly carved an inscription in the clay.

"What's this?" Freddy released her from his embrace and bent closer to read the words in the dim light of the lantern.

I love you, Plato.

As the meaning of her inscription began to register in Freddy's mind, Johanna said the words aloud in a fragile, breathy voice. "I love you, Plato."

Freddy sat back on his heels. *Plato*. The CB handle that connected him to his ten years as a long-haul trucker and to another persona—the man who'd had a passionate affair with Eastern and Western philosophy since his youth. Which man did Johanna see when she looked at him, loved him, inscribed these words in clay?

What did he have to offer a woman studying for her doctorate, a woman who wore heirloom pearls in her earlobes twenty-four hours a day? She may have grown up in tomboy tradition in the Ozarks, but Johanna was sophisticated, polished, fine-boned, and beautiful.

Freddy rested his palms against his jean-clad thighs and looked down at his callused fingertips. The second-generation son of an Italian taxidermist, he saw himself as exuberant, gesturing, earthy, and impulsive. Handsome perhaps, in a paste-pearl sort of way.

Perhaps dredging up these self-doubts would ease the pain of what he had to say.

"Johanna"—Freddy put his hands on her shoulders and found it hard to meet her gaze—"I have to insist that you leave tomorrow with the others. I'm going to follow behind in a few days, but it'd be risky for you to travel alone with me. I'm concerned enough about my own safety. I don't want to take any chances on your getting hurt."

The warm gray of her eyes hardened to gunmetal. The soft lines around her mouth were suddenly rigid.

"You don't want me to take a chance?" Johanna's tone was incredulous. "Freddy, I took the chance of getting hurt when I agreed to share this wagon with you . . . and later when I shared your bed." Reaching up, she brushed his hands off her shoulders and backed away from him in a near-crouch.

"Dammit, Freddy, if you haven't learned by now that I'm a woman strong enough and brave enough to take risks, you're blind! Hopelessly blind because you don't really know me! And it's obvious that you don't want to take the time to learn!"

Turning abruptly, she pulled the bedroll from its storage space. Johanna yanked on the strings with quick, angry, frustrated movements. The ties became knotted.

Wordlessly, Freddy moved toward her. "Here, let me help you with that."

"I can *do* it," Johanna insisted as she nimbly untangled the cords. "I won't have you playing the overprotective-male game with me."

Moving toward the back of the wagon, she snapped the bedroll open with a flick of her wrists. It unfurled over the planks, only to be stopped by Freddy's outstretched hand.

"You can be a real pain in the butt sometimes, Remington!" He flung the rest of the bedroll open. "I've had protective feelings since the moment I moved in with you! But I've suppressed them because you told me you wanted this journey to be a chance to *test* yourself."

Johanna recalled the promise she'd made to herself that first day. This was to be a voyage of self-discovery. "I m—meant it," she stammered.

"And what is it, Johanna, that you're testing?" Freddy demanded as he crawled toward her on the sleeping bag.

His question caught her off guard. "Well, at first, I

wanted to challenge my sense of rugged individualism—"

"History four-oh-one is down the hall. This is our wagon and we're—" His voice quieted. "We're talking in more human terms." He was kneeling less than a foot away. "And you're wrong, Joey." He shook his head. "Our time together has been limited, but I've come to understand you. I've collected every clue and studied it; the unfinished sentences, your laughter and facial expressions, the proud way you carry yourself, the wonderful way you give and take when we make love . . ." His fingertips traced the line of her jaw. "I've learned you, Joey."

Bending forward, Freddy brushed his lips against hers, then captured her mouth in a deeply probing kiss. With gentle pressure, he pulled her up on her knees and molded her body against his. She relaxed under his reassuring touch.

"This need to test yourself," he said against her trembling lips. "I sense that you're searching for an answer only I can give you. Am I right?"

"Partly." Johanna felt her throat go dry. "I wanted to find out two things about myself. Am I independent and courageous enough to face the physical and emotional hardships the pioneers encountered."

"And?"

Johanna rested her cheek against his shoulder. She was hesitant to speak the truth, but the pressure of his hand on her back was encouraging. "I wanted to know if I'm still capable of loving a man intensely, of giving my whole heart to another person without fear of—being hurt."

She heard his soft gasp. "I know you're brave,

Joey, but what about the rest? What have you discovered about love?"

"I love you, Freddy, but I can't give you my whole heart. Not after your speech. You hurt me tonight." Her throat burned with unshed tears.

He crushed her to his chest. "And I'm sorry. I wanted to give you a chance to leave with the others tomorrow graciously, without a public scene."

"I'm not leaving you, Freddy."

He pulled back. His dark eyes were questioning as he met her gaze. "You'll stay behind and love me with half a heart?" His fingers were on the buttons of her blouse.

"Yes, I guess that's one way you could put it. I am staying behind with you but don't pressure me. I told you I was testing myself. The t-test isn't over. Finding one or two answers sometimes raises more questions."

His hand stole inside her blouse and cupped her left breast. "Tell me..." His voice held a sensuous warning. "What half of your heart do I need to convince?"

"I gave Poco a bath last night, Mr. Rotini." Tiffany rubbed her cheek against the small dog's body. "Just the mouth part, but it was hard work. My mom said you were going to stay behind because you were in trouble." Tears clung to the small girl's lashes. "Can I tell you a secret?"

"Of course." Freddy knelt down beside her. "What is it, Tiffany?"

She whispered in his ear in the breathy voice of a frightened child. Freddy suppressed a smile as he listened to her words.

She finished with an apologetic half cry. "I'm sorry if I did anything that got you in trouble, Mr. Rotini." There was a catch in her throat as she backed away and gave the Chihuahua a kiss. "I'm gonna miss you . . . and Poco."

"Actually, Tiffany, you did me a favor in a way. But if it'll make you feel better, you might want to tell your mom and dad the truth." Freddy hugged the child and took Poco from her. "Thank you for teaching Poco the new tricks. You write to me, okay?"

In the distance, Freddy could hear Charlie Vishtek's cry of "Wagon Ho!" and smiled.

"Oh, I almost forgot." Tiffany frowned as she pulled an envelope out of the pocket of her overalls. "This is for you." The child turned and ran toward her wagon where her mother was urgently motioning her.

Johanna was stroking the dying embers in the center of camp, her back turned to the departing wagons. Freddy had witnessed her tearful farewell with Coni Cameron and other passengers shortly after breakfast, surprised by the depth of her emotion.

"I heard the 'Wagon Ho.' Was Tiffany the last of our good-byes?" she asked.

"Apparently not. Someone has left us a note." Freddy handed the envelope to Johanna and sat down beside her, settling Poco in his lap. "I'll let you do the honors."

Johanna tore the flap open and pulled out a notecard. "What the— You're not going to believe this. Chef James LaVish left us his recipe for lingonberry crêpes." She held the card up for Freddy to see, then shook a finger at Poco. "It's obvious some dogs can't be trusted around food!"

"You're wrong. Tiffany confessed everything to me." Freddy patted the Chihuahua on the head. "She took the lingonberries and shared them with Poco, thinking they were power pellets and would give her the strength of ten women. Needless to say, she's disappointed that she's left with the strength of a little girl this morning and can't do anything to help me."

"She can tell the truth."

"She will—eventually. I just hope Tiffany waits a few days."

"But Freddy, what about your honor? The passengers might think—"

"My honor is intact. Before the end of the trip, the passengers will understand everything. Charlie approached me early this morning." Freddy stretched his legs out until his boots were only inches from the campfire's dying embers. "He told me he'd had it with that son of his. It seems James has depended on nepotism all his life. That's why he was hired as cook on the wagon train in the first place, and evidently, our chef always got his way because Charlie never put his foot down. When I took over as wagon master, James was upset to see his father demoted, and he didn't want me telling him to change the menu."

"That explains the grudge. But what about the poker game and the accusations of cheating?"

"Charlie never believed I cheated in the first place and says his son forced him to agree to the rematch. Charlie decided to wear the dress to embarrass James, who is very concerned about appearances."

"But how is this going to give you back your honor if—"

"Don't worry, in a day or two, Charlie plans to teach James a real lesson."

"Hmmm, I wish I could see the fireworks." Johanna shook her head. "But in the meantime, we're left on our own . . ."

"I *want* this time alone with you, Johanna. Did it ever occur to you that I might want to *test* myself as well?"

"No." Johanna shook her head. "How do you intend to do that?"

"The first thing I want to do is harness the team and try driving this wagon down a few back roads. Maybe by the end of the day, we'll find an interesting little campsite where we can settle. Someplace private, close to water."

"With all of the amenities of home—you wish."

Freddy hesitated. "Johanna, I don't have a home. Spending the last week in this wagon with you has been the closest thing to home I've known in almost ten years."

"But where do you stay between truck hauls?"

"I keep a small room in the family home in Portland. When I'm in New Mexico, I stop in Taos to see my sister. I have friends and relatives across the country who let me use their couch in times of need."

"But everybody has a home."

"Are you sure? Where is yours, Johanna?"

"Yale—"

"Don't you live off campus?"

"In an apartment with my roommate, but that's not really home . . . yet. I have my goals."

"And there's a permanent home mixed with those goals?"

"Yes, of course. I plan to teach college-level history on a West Coast campus where I can do more research on the people who homesteaded along the way or made it to the end of the Oregon Trail."

"I could show you some beautiful places out west. I plan to settle back in Oregon, maybe go back to school for my doctorate there someday myself. Someday soon."

Silence followed his proclamation.

"But, you know. . ." Freddy smoothed the back of his hand over Johanna's slender throat, then reached up to caress the silky black waves that cascaded down her back. "We don't have to have a shingled roof over our heads to enjoy certain amenities." His hand moved down her back to the enticing curves that fit snugly into her jeans.

"Freddy!" Johanna scooted away and laughed playfully. "I thought we were going to harness the team." She scattered the embers in the campfire, then bent over to pick up a bucket of water. "I better make sure this fire is out before we leave."

Freddy stood and wrapped his arms around her from behind. "Keep bending over like that," he whispered, "and you'll rekindle all sorts of flames."

"It's not too late for me to run after the wagon train," she threatened. "And I happen to be holding a bucket of water that will douse any flame you claim to be kindling. We have work to do." Johanna's tone was adamant.

"All right." Freddy released her. "I'll get the livestock, you get the harness, and let's blaze our own trail."

* * *

"How bad is it?" Johanna asked, cupping her hand to shade her eyes from the bright overhead sun.

"Bad." She strained to hear Freddy's muffled response from beneath the wagon. "The wooden round part—"

"The felloe . . . that's like 'fellow' with an *e* on the end instead of a *w.*"

"Errr, the *felloe* is split, and two of the long wooden doohickeys—"

"Spokes."

"I knew that. Two of the spokes are snapped where they join the felloe. Can I just say that the back wheel is broken, Johanna?"

"Uh-huh. I can see that from here. What are you doing under the wagon?"

"Looking for the spare. I thought for sure there'd be one fastened under here."

"I doubt it. That's why people traveled in groups." Johanna straightened and turned in a complete circle as she tried to get her bearings. They were at the base of a steep rocky ravine close to a line of cottonwoods that bordered a creek. There was water and grazing for the team, and there'd be firewood and shade for the human beings in the party. But they were out of view of passing traffic, which would make their rescue difficult.

Freddy crawled out from under the wagon and dusted himself off. "Well, we learned one thing. You can't leave a couple of horses alone on a deserted country road while you sit in the grass and try to grab a little lunch."

"Put the blame where it should lie, Freddy." Johanna looked down at Poco. "First the lingonberries, now the horses. This Chihuahua is a j-i-n-x."

"He just barked a couple of times. I think he's upset about leaving the other wagons, and he misses Tiffany, no doubt." Freddy shook his head. "How are the horses? They seem to be calming down."

Johanna ran her hand soothingly along the flank of one animal. "I'm glad they're not hurt, but they're still a little shaken. Might as well take the harnesses off. We're not going anywhere today—or tomorrow—or possibly the following day. Do you have any idea where we are?"

They began the task of unharnessing the horses.

"You have the map Charlie gave us, don't you?" Freddy asked.

"What map?"

"The one he handed you this morning after breakfast."

"That was a map? I wrote my address on it for Coni Cameron and gave it to her." Johanna glanced at him over the rump of the horse on her side of the wagon.

"Okay, there's no need to get too concerned." Freddy smiled and rubbed his palms together. "Let's see. We don't have any saddles for the horses. Hmmm, the closest town must be twenty miles away, and I can't remember how far back the last farmhouse was—"

"About ten or twelve miles, I'd estimate," Johanna said with a shrug. "It's easier to guess mileage when you're in a car."

"I wouldn't chance trying to find our way back. I have no sense of direction."

"No sense of direction? How could you have been a truck driver?"

"Maps. Habit. Gas station attendants." Freddy rubbed his chin and seemed to ignore her question. "Even if we knew where we were, or if we could fix the back wheel, we wouldn't be able to get this wagon back up that incline to the road or through the trees and water to that field of— What is in that field?" He shaded his eyes.

"Rocks. Hills. More rocks. And tall grass." Johanna tried to keep her voice calm and level. This was hardly the idyllic romantic Sunday ride she had envisioned. "Freddy, we have food supplies that will last a week if we ration them, and we can build a fire signal. We're going to be all right."

Freddy busied himself hanging the harness neatly on the side of the wagon. His eyes were crinkled with amusement when he turned around to face her. "You, Johanna Remington, are the one who wanted to test your courage, and a few other capacities as well. I believe this is your dream come true, isn't it?" he asked with a mischievous smile as he pulled her into his arms. "I hope there's room for two in your dream this afternoon. That stream sounds very inviting, and later we can lie on the blanket and grab a little sun."

"You sound like some kind of social director—" Johanna's words were lost in the pleasure of his lips on hers.

"That last night in camp you wondered if you were still capable of loving a man intensely, Joey. What happened to make you doubt that?" Freddy asked, turning on his side in the sleeping bag.

Johanna smiled to herself in the dim light of the waning moon. She'd spent the past forty-eight-plus hours in constant togetherness with Freddy. They'd discussed everything from personal philosophy to favorite movies, from musical, literary, and culinary tastes to dreams and fantasies. And some of her secret fantasies had come alive in Freddy's arms.

If help didn't arrive soon, they'd burn off what little food they had rationed with all their nonwork activity. In desperation, she'd begun to read accounts of starvation aloud from the pioneers' diaries.

Turning toward Freddy, Johanna pondered his question for a moment. She'd known this area of her life—her past relationships with men—would eventually become part of their marathon discussion, but now hardly seemed the right time to dredge up bittersweet memories of Ronnie Buck. But would there ever be a better time?

Slowly, she began to unravel the story of her childhood in Missouri. Her family's small farm adjoined that of the Fergusons, and it was natural that Johanna and Ronnie Buck would grow up as playmates and friends. It was fate, perhaps, that had transformed the friendship into romance and plans of marriage after college. He had gone to Texas. She had won scholarships on the East Coast. And perhaps it was a twisted sort of fate that had allowed Ronnie Buck to abandon his promise to Johanna to marry his college sweetheart.

Freddy kissed her cheek gently. "You loved him with your whole heart and he hurt you, Joey. Are you telling me you'll never give that much of yourself to a man again? How can you measure your feelings like ingredients for a recipe?"

"I only wanted to be honest with you. I can give you my love, Freddy, but not my trust. Not yet. That's the half that holds me back."

He gathered her naked warmth against him, content to hold her as he searched for assurance. He could wait. He would earn her trust. He knew now that Johanna Remington was the woman he had searched for and dreamed of all those long nights on the road. Feeling her arms close around him calmed his gypsy soul and made him feel as though he'd come home at last.

CHAPTER NINE

FREDDY SAW THE horses perk up their ears long before the low pulsating roar became distinct, then loud. "Sounds like some sort of aircraft!" he shouted to Johanna as he set a bucket of feed on the ground. "Help me secure the team!" Freddy scrambled over the edge of the makeshift corral and tied one of the horses to a tree limb.

Minutes later, dust and debris swirled around the camp as a helicopter flew over the cottonwoods and came into view.

"Someone's found us!" Johanna's cry was lost in the roar of the blades overhead. She waved her arms frantically as she stumbled across the rocky ground toward Freddy and grabbed hold of his shirt.

The helicopter hovered for a moment, then circled and set down on the level road overlooking the ravine. An eerie quiet followed, broken by an occasional protest from the horses. Then Poco bounded out of the wagon and, barking wildly, ran nonstop up the steep incline.

"Oh, my God, it's Andee!" Freddy choked.

"Do you know the pilot?" Johanna paused. A small dark-haired woman emerged awkwardly from the passenger side, laughing, waving enthusiastically and holding a delirious Poco. It could mean only one thing. "Freddy, is that your sister, from Taos?"

"You bet. And this is just like her—conducting her own search and rescue." With a whoop, he began moving toward the embankment.

"But, Freddy, she's pregnant." Johanna hurried to catch up. "Very pregnant."

"Don't worry about it, Johanna. She's not due for another month or so, and she wouldn't have done this without asking her doctor." Freddy began climbing the hill just as his sister began descending. "Hey—" he called out. "Is that a good idea?"

"I'm fine," Andee reassured him with a laugh as she slid down the last foot of incline into his arms. "I'm glad to see you two are okay."

Johanna and Andee were quickly introduced. The accident that had caused the broken wagon wheel was recounted. The pilot made a few trips up and down the hill with feed for the horses, assorted food and drink for the humans, and a bag of hamburgers for Poco.

"Eat! Lord, you two must be starving." Andee hugged both Freddy and Johanna again. "You've been stuck here for more than five days."

"How did you find out?"

"Charlie Vishtek called. He said the wagon train arrived at the destination point and he stayed on waiting for you." Andee knelt on the blanket and began unpacking food. "When your wagon failed to show up after the expected two days, he got worried but didn't think it was time to call out the search-and-rescue units. So I called Thor—"

"Her photographer husband," Freddy interjected.

"I called Thor in Utah where he's shooting a magazine spread and left a message for him, then last night I flew to the closest city and hired a helicopter and pilot. This morning Cory and I started searching down every back road while I prayed to Saint Anthony."

"He's the patron saint of lost objects," Freddy explained to Johanna.

She nodded. "I'm impressed—with Saint Anthony. What happens now?"

"Cory will fly back to the airport," Andee explained between bites of fried chicken, "and he'll call Thor with the good news and contact Charlie Vishtek, who will probably want to help salvage your wagon. It looks like it might be a delicate operation—"

"And we'll all wait here for Thor?" Johanna asked anxiously. When Andee nodded, Johanna felt apprehensive. "But what about you . . . isn't the baby . . . aren't you going back where you'll be close to a hospital?"

"No, the baby isn't due for six weeks. It'll be fun to spend the night here." Andee spread her arms. "I love adventures—hiking, camping, whatever."

"I don't think spending the night is such a great idea, Andee." Freddy cleared his throat. "We only have one sleeping bag."

"Don't worry, I brought blankets and bedrolls." His sister spoke slowly as she studied him for a long moment, then shifted her gaze to Johanna. "So you two—I don't suppose you've been taking turns using this one sleeping bag?"

"No," Johanna said with a laugh. "We sleep together . . . in the same bedroll. Didn't Charlie Vishtek say anything to you about Freddy staying in my wagon?"

"No, he didn't mention anything about a romance." Andee leaned toward Johanna. "But he had an interesting story to tell about a near-mutiny over some misunderstanding about blackberries—"

"Lingonberries," Freddy corrected.

"Oh, yes. Thor's favorite. Well, that makes more sense now. . ." Andee ruminated. "Anyway, that was the first mutiny."

"What else did Charlie say?" Johanna prompted. "What's happened?"

"A little girl confessed that she took the berries and fed them to Poco," Andee continued. "Seems there was a second revolt in the camp, and—I'm not real clear about this—Charlie said the crew and passengers took off his *dress* and forced his son to wear it? And this Charlie fellow actually seemed happy about it. Could that be correct? Sounds a little kinky to me."

"No, Andee," Freddy threw back his head and joined in Johanna's laughter. "It sounds like pioneer justice to me! Charlie Vishtek got around to teaching his son a lesson."

"Maybe it's—false labor or heartburn," Andee suggested to Freddy when the first pain struck two hours after the pilot left.

"Wait here on the blanket and stay calm," Freddy

ordered. "Johanna's taking a bath in the stream. She grew up on a farm in the Ozarks, Andee. Maybe she knows something about . . . all this birthing business."

"Johanna," Freddy called as he arrived breathlessly at the stream, "it's Andee—she's had a strong pain. Just one, Joey, but it could be a contraction."

Johanna felt like sinking beneath the surface of the stream and pretending she hadn't heard his words. Panic rose in her being, moving like fine lacework through her limbs.

"I can't . . . never again . . . please don't make me!" The words were pouring out of her mouth in a senseless, traitorous fashion. The water that had seemed so warm a moment ago was chilling her to the bone. Her muscles spasmed and she felt her scalp tingling.

"What's wrong?" She heard Freddy's voice and felt his arms move around her. Taking off his shirt, he wrapped it over her shoulders. "You're shivering. Come out of the water and tell me what's wrong."

Johanna stumbled up the embankment. "If it's the baby, I c-can't help you, Freddy. My God! Don't you see? I—I . . . killed my brother—please, please, don't make me help." She heard herself ranting, saw herself gesturing, and was hopeless in her attempts to control herself. He grabbed the towels and began to dry her body.

"Keep talking, Johanna. I don't understand half of what you're saying, but keep talking," Freddy urged as he struggled to pull her jeans over each foot and dress her. "What happened? Tell me about it."

"Mama was seven months pregnant, and we were alone in the cabin. Daddy was selling livestock in the next county. The storm hit and we were all alone." Johanna heard herself speaking more clearly and wished the words would jumble again. The memory was too painful to recall in detail.

"What happened, Joey? Don't hold it in. Come on, tell me." Freddy layered her with a blouse and warm-up jacket.

"During the storm . . . the water overflowed the banks. The bridge was gone. Mama and I tried to stay calm. We were making soup . . . and then the pains started. The baby was coming. I didn't know what to do. No phone to call the doctor. No power." The words were coming faster, clear now. Freddy kissed her cheek as he dried her hair and urged her to remember.

"I'd never seen my mama cry or scream before. She was always such a calm woman, but she started screaming at me and—begging me to help her." Johanna broke into a sob. "Oh, my God, that tiny little baby. I didn't know what to do. Find clothes and blankets and keep everyone else warm. My hands . . . the cabin smelled like onions—we were making the soup. Maybe it was the onions—"

"Joey, Joey." Freddy was rocking her in his arms, whispering her name over and over as he tried to reassure her. "It wasn't your fault."

"I did everything Mama told me to . . . but she wasn't making sense half the time. I boiled the scissors and tied off the cord and then he—he opened his little eyes, Freddy. My brother looked up at me. Oh God, oh God, he had such forgiving eyes. He hardly made a sound."

The memory was a hot ember she had tried to extinguish for more than half of her life. Recounting the scene was like throwing cold water on those coals. The steam rolled through her mind, blinding her, then clearing and revealing details she had sought to forget. Johanna was choked with racking sobs. Freddy's words reached through the fog to comfort her, but the pain was searing.

"Mama didn't say so but I've known all these years that I could have saved him, Freddy. There had to be a way. If only I had known. If only I had stayed calm, but I must have panicked. I killed h—him."

"Shhhh." Freddy was speechless. How could he possibly reassure her? All he could do was ask questions. "How long did he live, Joey?"

"For a—about an hour after he was born, I suppose."

"And your mother was all right? She was lucky you were there for her. You could have lost them both."

"Mama recovered slowly, but she never talked about the baby or the things that happened that night. My father told me later, when I was older, that my mother had lost other children early in pregnancy." Johanna's cheek was pressed against Freddy's bare chest. Her sobs subsided. "Mama was depressed for what seemed like years. Little things upset her, and she was always worrying about where I was and what I was doing. The warmth we had shared was gone. Mama seemed empty all the time. I—I thought she was angry with me—"

Freddy cradled Johanna in his arms and rocked her while he let his own tears flow freely. How could he ask Johanna to help his sister? What if—no, he wouldn't give power to negative thoughts. Andee's baby would be fine. His sister was healthy. People frequently had babies at home.

"How old were you, Joey, when . . . when this happened?"

"Eleven," she answered in a choked whisper. "My God, I hadn't even started having periods yet."

He touched her gently, brushing his hand over her cheek, kissing her temple, making soft cooing sounds, wishing he could absorb her pain. "How are you feeling?"

"Better . . . in some ways. I've never told anyone before."

Was she learning to trust him? Freddy recalled the discussion they'd had before leaving camp. He wasn't going to do anything that might destroy this fragile foundation.

"Johanna, I—I'd better check on Andee. I don't feel I have the right to ask you to help if she *is* in labor. Maybe the pilot will come back soon. And then again Andee said it could be something as simple as heartburn. I don't know—I'm a little frightened about this. I don't know anything at all about babies. My brother Alberto is a gynecologist. Andee chose the wrong relative—"

Johanna took a deep breath, agonizing over her decision. Seeing Freddy's pain and helplessness was unbearable. She knew he was close to Andee. The sister and brother had spent three summers driving the truck together. Fresh tears sprang to her eyes as she thought about her lonely childhood and pondered for a moment the kind of relationship she might have shared with a sibling.

With trembling fingers, Johanna bent over to pick up her hairbrush, praying that there was a simple explanation for the pain Andee had experienced. An explanation other than labor. "Freddy, when you talk to your sister, please don't tell her about my mother and the baby. There's no need to upset her."

As Johanna swung her hair back and began to untangle the waves, she looked up and saw the remnant of tears on Freddy's cheeks. She wiped the moisture away with a fingertip and gave him a faint smile. "My tears ended up on your face. I must be a mess—"

"They were *my* tears, Joey," Freddy said softly. His eyes were warm and adoring. "I'm sorry you had to suffer through anything that traumatic at such a tender age." His arms moved around her.

The realization that Freddy had been moved to tears stirred another part of her painful memory. Johanna's throat ached as she recalled her father's homecoming the day after the storm. Joe Remington was a tall, muscular man not given to displays of emotion.

Her mother had been sleeping soundly. Exhausted and distraught, eleven-year-old Johanna met her father at the door. Fighting back tears, she helped him out of his wet slicker and boots, halfheartedly listening to his account of having to detour around the washed-out bridge.

When her father sat down in the chair by the door to pull off his wet socks, Johanna crumpled against his broad chest and sobbed out the story. He held her tightly against him until she calmed. After looking in on his sleeping wife, her father came out of the bedroom, embraced Johanna, and told her that he was going to hold the baby for a moment before taking him into town for burial in the churchyard.

The heartwrenching picture remained intact in her memory. Joe Remington had gazed into the restful features of his baby son and then, in a choked voice, named him Henry. The evening before, Johanna had seen her mother cry for the first time. Less than twenty-four hours later, her father sat in the rocking chair by the wood stove, tears of grief glistening on his cheeks.

Johanna felt a surge of empathy for Andee and Thor. This might be an emergency. After witnessing her parents' grief, how could she refuse to help?

Freddy brushed his lips against her forehead. "I better go back to camp to see how Andee's doing. I know you don't like overprotective men, Johanna, but I wish you'd lean on me more often."

"If Andee *is* in labor, Freddy, I'll do that."

"What do you mean?"

"I'm going to help your sister."

"How's she feeling?" Freddy stood anxiously outside the wagon where they'd arranged a bed of sorts for Andee.

"She's calm and resting, singing softly to Poco. I read to her from the pioneer journals for a bit—there are some accounts of rather courageous births in there." Johanna let out a long sigh. "I wish that pilot would get back."

"I know." Shading his eyes, Freddy examined the clear blue prairie sky. "I've been trying to recall all those reruns of *Wagon Train* I watched after I won the poker game. There were babies, but there wasn't any helpful detail." Freddy folded his arms against his chest and leaned back against the wagon. "I'm boiling water."

"Oh, good." Johanna smiled. "I could use a cup of strong tea."

"You're acting rather calm about this," Freddy observed as he grabbed two metal cups.

"I want Andee to stay calm. I've gathered all the linens and towels I could find. We're lucky she brought the sheets and blankets along." Johanna proceeded to list a number of problems and their seemingly easy solutions in a staid voice.

The sound of an engine interrupted her musings. Both Johanna and Freddy looked up, searching for a helicopter but finding none. There was a shout and they turned in unison to stare at the road above the ravine. A man was climbing out of a Jeep emblazoned with the words BOB'S RENTALS.

"It's Thor!" Freddy said with relief.

"I had a feeling that anyone who looked like that had to be Thor Engborg," Johanna muttered as she studied the tall, muscular blond male dressed in safari wear and jackrabbiting down the steep incline in hiking boots.

Introductions were cut short by Thor's persistent quesiton. "Where's Andee?"

The man's cool demeanor was shattered by the announcement that his wife was inside the wagon... and in labor.

"She shouldn't have left Taos. Are you sure the baby is coming? Is it too late to drive her to the nearest town?" Thor's inquiries lasted the length of the rocky pasture.

"Thor, where's the helicopter?" Freddy interrupted.

"The pilot had a medical emergency that took priority. He'll be here as soon as he's finished. I hope that's soon!"

Five minutes later, after assessing the situation,

Thor reverted to his native Norwegian tongue and proved to be about as helpful as Poco, who'd had to be forcibly removed from Andee's bedside.

"Have you taken the childbirth classes? Do you remember anything?" Johanna asked Thor bluntly.

"*Ja.*"

"Well, what do you remember?" she prompted.

"Stay calm."

"How many classes have you attended?"

"Two. I travel a lot . . . but I read the books. The photographs were very well done. I was very impressed with the photography."

Johanna threw up her hands and turned to Freddy. He was kneeling just inside the wagon helping Andee with her breathing. "One monkey, two monkey, three monkey—"

"Freddy, don't make me laugh!" Andee cried.

"I can't help it. Johanna and I have both lost our watches in the stream these past few days. I haven't got anything but monkeys to offer you," he explained in his most comforting tone. When Andee began laughing again, he backed away. "I better boil more water—for tea."

As the afternoon shadows lengthened, Johanna entered the wagon for the last time. With soft words and reassuring touches, she coached Andee through the contractions, following instinct and vague recollections from pioneer journals. Ripping a strip of fabric from the bottom of her blouse, she tied it around her forehead to catch the falling perspiration. A panic-stricken Thor spent much of the time hyperventilating into a paper sack while Freddy boiled scissors, knives, and every metal object he could find.

Johanna fought her private fears and anguished memories, setting them aside to concentrate on assisting Andee. The final moments of childbirth were punctuated by encouragement in Norwegian by Thor, Italian by Freddy, English by Johanna, and an occasional bark from Poco.

The tiny dark-haired baby girl that Johanna Remington handed to Andee minutes after the birth seemed unaware of her prairie birthing room or any language barriers as she began to nurse cooperatively at her mother's breast.

"We're alone with our stars again, Joey." Freddy walked up behind Johanna and put his arms around her waist. She'd been oddly quiet since Thor, Andee, and Hanna Katrina Engborg had been airlifted by the helicopter pilot to a nearby hospital. Johanna and Freddy had agreed to stay with the horses, Poco, and the wagon until Charlie Vishtek arrived the following day.

"This might be our last night together, Freddy," Johanna said quietly.

"Impossible," he whispered into the side of her neck. "Not with all that star seed up there for us to wish on. Perhaps it's harvest time."

"And what kind of wishes do you want to harvest, Mr. Rotini?" She turned in his arms to face him.

"Only the ones you can grant me, Johanna." He rested his forehead against hers and sighed. "Can I tell you one more time? You were fantastic today . . . holding all of us together through the labor and the birth. If you want to write about courage in your thesis, Joey, turn inward and examine the person you are."

"Correction." Johanna put a finger against his lips. "The person I became *today.* When I watched that little baby—Hanna—arrive, I discovered the self I've been looking for throughout this journey, throughout my adult life perhaps. I don't want to test myself anymore, Freddy. I don't need to. In a few more months, I'll break free of the walls of academia, and I'll face the real world."

She slipped her finger off his lips, replacing it with the pressure of her mouth on his. Her voice was breathless when she spoke. "You mentioned wishes? What do you want, Freddy?"

His hands strayed to her breast. "The half of your heart you weren't sure of . . . and your trust."

"That wish was granted long ago. I just didn't realize it until now."

"You mean I wasted a perfectly good wish? How many do I get?"

"One for every star you can see, of course."

Freddy glanced up at the vast prairie sky. He felt a strange heat move through his chest and invade his limbs. "I'm going to give Charlie Vishtek full partnership with me on the wagon train, whether he likes it or not. Only this time, he'll be wagon master and I'll play mule skinner and bullwhacker while I learn the ropes—the hard way, like anyone else."

Freddy moved downward to the sleeping bag, pulling her with him. "Then I'm returning to school. I want to teach college-level philosophy during the school year and spend my summers working on the RIDE THE OREGON TRAIL WAGON TREK."

Johanna raised an eyebrow. Where did she fit into this plan? she wondered. "Maybe we'll teach at the same college—"

"I don't want *maybe*, Joey. I'm going to be working with ropes and knots for the rest of my life. Right now I want to tie the most important knot of my life—with you. How do you feel about spending your summers on the Oregon Trail with a former truck driver named Plato?"

"Hmmm, something tells me this is going to be a very good harvest." Johanna skimmed her fingers over the edge of his jawline.

"A bumper crop of star seed, Ms. Remington."

"Do you realize that in all this time we haven't had a chance to discuss Manifest Destiny?" she asked as his fingers unzipped her velour top.

"If we were marooned out here for thirty years, I doubt if we'd have time to even touch upon the subject," Freddy replied dryly.

EPILOGUE

TRAVEL THE OREGON TRAIL!

Ten action-packed days of adventure on the Oregon Trail. Follow the path of pioneers in a covered wagon! Enjoy cookouts, square dancing, horseback riding, history lessons, hiking, and fishing. Sing songs and share folklore. Our philosophy is one of fun! Meet wagon master and storyteller Charlie Vishtek. Meals prepared by Chef James LaVish, author of *The Oregon Trail Cookbook*. For brochures, applications, and more information, write to wagon-masters-in-training Freddy and Johanna Rotini c/o Pacific University, Forest Grove, Oregon.

COMING NEXT MONTH

A LADY'S CHOICE #432
by Cait Logan

Emily Northrup returns to her rural hometown to nurse an ailing aunt and clashes with her aunt's sexy neighbor, Cal McDonald. Cal's fascinated Emily since her teen-age years, and their passion explodes as the townspeople place bets on their wedding date...

CLOSE SCRUTINY #433
by Pat Dalton

F.B.I. agent Niera Pascotti has lived dangerously while loving cautiously—until a mandatory vacation to Tahiti throws her into the arms of mysterious Cort Tucker. Niera can't resist Cort, yet she must discover his identity while masking her own...